SPECTRE: ORIGINS

The *SPECTRE RISING* PREQUEL SERIES

C.W. LEMOINE

SPECTRE: ORIGINS

Copyright 2013 C.W. Lemoine

Table of Contents

Author's Note

SPECTRE: ORIGINS is a collection of short stories from the lives of the main characters of my new book **SPECTRE RISING**. It is intended to be a prequel series that gives a look into the history and past of some of the main characters.

Although some of the stories are based on real events, the narrative is entirely fiction. The squadrons and people in this eBook are invented. Actual operational squadrons and places were used only to enhance the realism and credibility of the story.

The views in this book are entirely my own, and do not represent those of the United States Air Force Reserve or United States Navy Reserve.

I've also included a sample of my book SPECTRE RISING. I hope after reading these short stories, you'll join me in the adventures of Cal "Spectre" Martin and his friends. Thanks for reading.

Marcus Anderson

Hero's Unwelcome

30KM West of Sarajevo
1 February 1996

He had been deployed as part of a peacekeeping force. At least, that's what the media had been told. But Gunnery Sergeant Marcus Anderson knew that the only peacekeeping he did was from behind his scope. And as he lay quietly in the brush on the snow-covered hilltop, covered by his arctic camouflage ghillie suit, Marcus secretly hoped that they would cancel the mission and send him home. He had seen enough war for one lifetime.

Marcus had enlisted in the Marine Corps during the height of the Reagan military buildup. He had worked his way through the ranks, first as a basic infantryman, then achieving a slot in the coveted Marine Scout Sniper School shortly after pinning on the rank of Lance Corporal. He had always been proficient with firearms, having been taught at a young age by his father, a long time veteran of the Miami Police Department. Shooting was just a natural thing for Marcus.

This was his third combat deployment, and Marcus was seeing the light at the end of the tunnel. He had spent months waiting for the green light in Iraq during Desert Shield, and eventually chased down Iraqi Republican Guard commanders and mobile SCUD launchers in the deserts of Iraq during Desert storm. He had hunted and killed Somali warlords in Mogadishu in 1993, an operation he considered to be successful despite what the media had portrayed after nineteen brave Army Rangers and Delta Operators had been killed after a Blackhawk was shot down. And now he found himself back in the action again, hunting down Serbian commanders guilty of heinous war crimes.

He lay prone, concealed by thick brush and the woods on the top of the small hill. His spotter, Corporal Matt Bynes lay next to him. It was their fifth mission in Bosnia over the last three months, and Marcus had been assured by his Captain that things were starting to wind down and that they would be headed back to the states soon. Marcus wasn't sure he believed it, but he certainly wasn't going to argue if that were true. His wife was still waiting for him back home. At least, he hoped she was. He hadn't received a letter from her in a couple of weeks, and she never seemed to be around or able to talk when he called.

"I've got the mark," Bynes said as he peered through his binoculars. Bynes was over a decade younger than Marcus who was pushing his late thirties. They had been paired for this deployment - the crusty old Gunny taking the young Corporal under his wing. Marcus' only goal was to get them both home alive. Anything beyond that was a bonus.

"Crossing the road?" Marcus said as he picked up the man through the scope of his M40A1 rifle chambered in 7.62 x 51 NATO. The man was a Serbian Colonel that had been responsible for shelling a small village outside of Sarajevo. He was wearing a Serbian military winter uniform, escorted by a small contingent of soldiers. They had been watching the target area for the last two days, having received intel that he had set up his base of operations amongst a small village to discourage NATO allied bombings.

"Affirm, 564 yards, winds out of the east, two miles per hour," Bynes responded as he confirmed Marcus' calculations for windage, drop, and density. At that range, the smallest error would be the difference between a kill shot and exposing their position with nothing to show for it.

Marcus clicked in the settings in his scope as he zeroed his sights on the man's head. That was the life of a sniper - hours, even days, of sitting and waiting followed by intense, split second, life and death decision-making. His adrenaline was pumping, but he remained unphased. He now only had to focus on his breathing and trigger pull as the man stood talking to one of his Lieutenants.

"Target confirmed, cleared to engage," Bynes whispered.

Marcus took a deep breath and exhaled slowly. His warm breath condensed in the cold, dry winter air. With a smooth trigger pull, Marcus sent the round downrange. The bullet hit the Colonel in the temple mid-sentence, instantly dropping him to the ground as brain matter splattered the officer next to him. The men were sent in a frenzy as they scattered to seek cover and blindly returned fire.

Marcus and his spotter maintained their cover, careful not to make any movements or sounds to give away their position. At that range, there was no way the panicking officers would be able to locate their position from the single gunshot. All Marcus and his spotter needed to do now was wait for the dust to settle as stray, unaimed rounds ripped at tree limbs beneath them and sent snow flying. A few minutes later, the gunfire stopped as the men dragged the Colonel's body out of the street and a patrol started up the hillside to their right.

Marcus froze as he heard a tree limb crack to his left. It hadn't been a round striking the trees, but someone stepping on an old branch in the snow. He and Bynes had scouted the area pretty well before settling on their current OP, but random foot patrols were not uncommon either. Marcus snaked his hand down to his Beretta 92FS sidearm.

"Get ready to move, kid," Marcus whispered as the footsteps grew near. Bynes readied his handgun as well, trying to remain perfectly still. They would lay in wait, hoping the soldiers would walk past them.

As the footsteps drew nearer, Marcus could finally see who had been making the noise. They were two men, each appearing to be in their mid-twenties, carrying AK-47s slung from their necks. Marcus clenched the butt of his Beretta as the men approached. They didn't appear to have noticed Marcus and his spotter, but they were on track to stumble over them.

The two men were within twenty feet of Marcus and Bynes. Marcus hated the idea of shooting them in broad daylight without silenced weapons. Their position would immediately be given away to the other patrol. Suddenly, the men stopped. The lead man motioned for them to turn toward the village below them. Marcus breathed a sigh of relief as they changed course.

They walked a few feet and stopped. Marcus watched as the younger looking guard pulled a pack of cigarettes out of his pocket, offered one to his comrade, and they both lit up.

With their backs to him, Marcus unsheathed his boot knife. He didn't have time to wait. Their ride, a Marine UH-1 Huey, would be at the rendezvous point in two hours. They had a lot of ground to cover while avoiding enemy contact.

Following Marcus' lead, Bynes pulled out his knife and followed, approaching the soldier to the right. In unison, they both grabbed their respective guards, shoving their knives into the men's necks while covering their victims' mouths with their free hands. Once they were sure the men were dead, they dragged them off into the brush. *It was time to move.*

Making slow and deliberate movements, the two made their way over the hill toward the "military crest" of the mountain next to them. Staying three quarters of the way up the mountain allowed them to avoid enemy movements while maintaining a good tactical advantage and concealment. An hour and a half later, they were in position, hiding in the wooded area that opened to a clearing as they waited on their ride home.

"So how does it feel?" Bynes whispered.

"How does what feel?" Marcus asked impatiently. "It's fucking cold." A native of South Florida, Marcus hated cold weather. He was looking forward to the day he could retire on his houseboat in the Florida Keys and throw away all of his winter clothes in favor of flip flops and shorts.

"No, I mean how does it feel to be done?" Bynes pressed.

"We're not done until we're home, now shut the fuck up," Marcus grunted.

*****

It was just after 8PM when Marcus finally made it to

his truck in the deployment parking area. As Marcus made the final turn onto the base housing road in his 1994 Ford Bronco, he breathed a sigh of relief. After three days of going from base to base in Europe on his way back to Quantico, he was finally home.

It was Valentine's Day, three days before he had originally been scheduled to return. His Captain had given him a three-day pass in honor of his upcoming retirement and distinguished service. He was hoping to show up and surprise his wife, spending the weekend getting reacquainted after a long time apart.

Marcus had married Rhonda Myers just a year before his assignment to Quantico. She had been a hairdresser at a local salon near Yuma MCAS. They met at a bar outside of Yuma, Arizona and were married six months later. They had no children, but on his flight home from war-torn Bosnia, he had been thinking about kids. He had always told her he was too old, but now that he was leaving the Corps and settling down, he was starting to reconsider. Besides, she was still in her early twenties. She wasn't too old, regardless of how he felt about himself.

Marcus noticed an extra car on the street as he pulled into his duplex driveway next to Rhonda's Chevy Cavalier. He guessed it must've been his neighbors. He figured he'd have to have a talk with them about parking on his side of the lot, but for now, he was just looking forward to seeing Rhonda. He laughed at the "Clinton/Gore '96" sticker on the back windshield. It was ironic to Marcus that a person on a military base was supporting the same two politicians that had been doing their best to gut the military.

"Democrats," he chuckled to himself as he shook his head.

He started to pull out his keys but then decided to try the door. Despite his warnings that it was unsafe, Rhonda always left the door unlocked, even when she was alone. He twisted the doorknob and pushed. The deadbolt was locked. *Maybe she finally listened*, he thought. Marcus fished out his house keys and unlocked the door. He tossed his sea bag near the front door and looked around. The house was quiet.

"Rhonda?" Marcus called out. There was no response. Marcus looked in the kitchen. There were empty takeout boxes in the trash, but the kitchen was relatively clean. *Maybe she had changed while he had been gone.*

Marcus turned toward the stairs. He slowly made his way up as the wooden stairs creaked on every step. He could hear noises coming from their bedroom. It sounded like she was up watching TV.

"Guess who's-" Marcus stopped in his tracks as he opened the door. The TV was off, but there was his wife, on all fours, being mounted by another man like a dog in heat. They were both naked except for the man-he was wearing Marcus' boonie hat.

"Oh my God!" Rhonda screamed as she jumped up and covered herself with a stray pillow. Her lover just stood there naked, frozen by fear as he contemplated his fight or flight instinct.

Marcus took a step forward, his fists clenched, "YN1 Herrington." He recognized the offender. He was an admin clerk with the Navy. Herrington had helped process his travel claim on his last TDY before he left for Bosnia, and now he was violating his wife in his house and in his bed. Herrington's car had been the one parked out front.

Suddenly the man leapt forward, choosing fight over flight. His right arm swung wildly at Marcus as Marcus stepped back and ducked, sending the man stumbling away naked under his own momentum.

"You've got the nerve to try to fight me after you've been fucking my wife?" Marcus growled. "And wearing my goddamned hat?"

"She told me what a piece of shit you are!" Herrington yelled as he gathered himself and prepared to reattack.

Marcus gave Rhonda a look of betrayal. He had been gone for three months, serving his country the best way he knew how, and providing for her while she sat at home and lived a relatively comfortable life. *Her repayment was to fuck this guy? An admin weenie?*

"I suggest you put your fucking clothes back on and go home before you get hurt," Marcus said to Herrington as he waited for any explanation at all from Rhonda.

"Fuck you!" Herrington said as he charged Marcus. Again, he swung wildly as he neared Marcus. Marcus took another step back and redirected Herrington's momentum into the dresser. Pictures and a jewelry box went crashing to the floor.

"Marcus, Jacob, please!" Rhonda pleaded.

"This asshole doesn't deserve you!" Herrington yelled as he gathered himself up a third time.

Marcus finally lost his patience as the man picked himself back up. As the man steadied himself, Marcus jabbed his throat, careful not to crush his windpipe, but enough to make him gasp for air. As he doubled over, Marcus threw an elbow to the man's jaw, dislocating it instantly. He grabbed the man by the back of the neck and sent him head first into the dresser. Blood gushed from the man's broken nose as he writhed in pain.

"A fucking Democrat, Rhonda? Seriously?" Marcus said as the man rolled in pain. "You cheated on me with this pussy? Are you a lesbian now?"

"Marcus you were always gone!" Rhonda screamed.

"Whatever. Pack your shit and get out!" Marcus screamed.

Marcus had survived three conflicts, having been shot at, bombed, and forced to survive on his own for days in the wilderness, but Rhonda's betrayal hurt him the most. He had never felt so vulnerable before. YN1 Herrington spent two days in the hospital while Marcus' superiors tried their best to keep him out of the Brig by settling for a reduction in rank and forfeiture of pay, but the damage was done. Marcus vowed to never let himself be so vulnerable again.

Victor Alvarez

New Friends

Miami, FL
15 March 2007

"You're much better than he is," she said, rubbing the black hair on his chest.

Victor Alvarez sat up and swung his feet over the side of the bed. He looked over at her. She was laying there naked and sweating from their second lovemaking session of the evening. Her long, dark brown hair just barely covered her exposed breasts.

"We've got time for one more," she said as she sat up and kissed his neck.

Victor brushed his hands through his jet black hair. *These women always seemed to get so clingy.* "What time will he be home?"

"It's Thursday night. Jay goes to the track on Thursday nights," she said as she caressed his back.

"There will be more time for us later," he said as he turned to kiss her. She grabbed his face and kissed him sensually.

"When are we going to run away together like you promised? I've already started talking to divorce lawyers," she said. Her brown eyes were deep with concern. He had been working her for the past two months. On the other hand, maybe she had been working him. He had trouble thinking of it as "work."

"Soon, my love," he said, kissing her forehead, "but for now, I should go so as not to make a scene when he returns."

Victor stood, grabbing his pants and shirt from the foot of the bed. The woman crawled out of bed behind him. He took a moment to take in her toned body and caramel skin. He loved this job so much.

"Give me a moment and I'll walk you out," she said as she grabbed her robe and wrapped it around her.

Victor smiled as he continued putting on his clothes. As she walked into the bathroom, he slowly eased toward the dresser. Next to it sat a dirty clothes bin. When she was safely out of view, he carefully searched the drawers. *Nothing.* He looked into the dirty clothes and found a pair of men's slacks. He picked them up and dug through the pockets, pulling out two pieces of paper.

Victor glanced back to the bathroom as he opened the two crumpled pieces of paper. The first was an ATM receipt. Nothing unusual - just a one hundred dollar transfer. The second was a betting slip for the Flagler Greyhound Track in Miami.

Victor smiled as he stuffed the papers back in the pants and then put them back into the clothes bin. He had what he needed.

*****

"Rubio says this guy is ten grand in the hole," the man said as he sat next to Alvarez. It was Jose Herrera, his most trusted asset in Miami. Jose was a native of Miami. His parents had set their roots in Hialeah in the late sixties after fleeing Cuba, and although he didn't officially work for the Cuban DGI, he was very much on their payrolls.

The Dirección General de Inteligencia was the main state intelligence agency of Cuba. Since opening for business in late 1961, the DGI had been involved in intelligence and espionage operations across the globe. They had been involved in aiding leftist revolutionary movements in Africa, the Middle East, and mostly Latin America. In the United States, the DGI had been heavily involved with international drug trade, assisting homegrown terrorist cells, and intelligence gathering operations for third party countries.

"Total?" Alvarez asked as he watched the greyhounds speed by on the track. He was wearing a white button down shirt and straw fedora with khaki slacks.

"This month," Jose replied.

Alvarez put down his binoculars and looked at Jose. He had been using them to search for his target in the opposite stands. He knew the man would be there. It was Thursday night, after all.

"Rubio must appreciate that," Victor replied. Juan Rubio was one of the most vicious bookies in South Florida. He was known for extracting money from his clients at any cost and with his ties to the Latin Kings gang, he was immune from retribution or prosecution. No one dared to cross him.

"He already owes Rubio five grand," Jose said, lowering his voice, "Rubio's giving this guy just enough rope to hang himself."

Alvarez chuckled as he went back to his binoculars. He scanned the crowd in the stands across from them looking for his target.

"So he has the same plan we do," Victor said as he watched the man wearing shorts and a blue polo shirt. It was Special Agent Jay Leon, the new agent assigned to the Foreign Intelligence/Espionage desk of the Miami Field Office of the FBI.

Jose shrugged, "Do you want me to talk to him, boss?"

"See how much money it will take to buy him out," Alvarez responded. "I'm going to have a chat with our new friend."

*****

Victor Alvarez waited patiently in the dark corner of the VIP room of the club. Strip clubs were ideal for meetings like this, especially the VIP room. The loud music and dark rooms made it harder for people to eavesdrop. People rarely paid attention to anything but the girls, and no one gave a second glance to suspicious activity.

But Victor's target had no idea they were meeting. Victor's presence in the corner of the little strip club was the culmination of months of work spent selecting the target, working his way in, and finding his leverage.

A mid-level agent in the DGI, Victor Alvarez had spent his entire career working South Florida. He had served his country by building a network of intelligence assets throughout the local community. If a foreign country had an operation in Miami, he was their man. He was proud of the work he had done. He was known as one of the agency's most effective operatives, especially when it came to developing assets in government organizations. His superiors were always impressed at how he managed to turn even the most difficult targets into productive intelligence assets.

Special Agent Jay Leon was a project Victor's own government had given him. They had control of most of the local police departments, but their presence with the local feds was minimal at best. They only had low-level analysts who could feed them information if they happened upon it. They needed someone with a hand in Federal investigations. The man would be their eyes and ears, and if necessary, divert attention from whatever operations they were working.

So when Victor learned that the Foreign Intelligence

desk of the FBI was going to a new transfer originally from the area, he knew he would have his opportunity. Leon's father still lived in Cuba. He could be used as leverage if necessary, Victor had thought.

It hadn't been necessary. Victor worked it the best way he knew how – in the bedroom. He watched Leon and his wife over the course of several weeks. They had no kids. She was a bored housewife following her husband from assignment to assignment. He could work with that.

And he did. *Over and over again.* He promised her adventure and excitement. He promised her a new life and a romantic getaway. It was all a lie, of course, but it had gotten him close enough to get the information he needed. He didn't feel bad. She could do better than Leon anyway. Leon apparently had a gambling problem, and judging by his frequent trips to the establishment Victor was sitting in, a fidelity problem as well.

Victor sat back as he watched a stripper guide Leon up the stairs and onto one of the couches. She kissed his cheek and walked away, promising that his girl would be up shortly.

Leon looked around for a second, and then began to unzip his pants.

"Keep your pants on," Alvarez said from the corner.

Startled, Leon jumped up, holding his pants.

"Who the fuck are you?" he demanded. "Where's Candy?"

"Prostitution is illegal in Florida, Mr. Leon," Alvarez

said smoothly.

"I said who the fuck are you?" Leon demanded, zipping his pants. "How do you know my name?"

"I know everything about you, Special Agent Leon. Please sit down. Let's chat."

Alvarez sat patiently as Leon approached. "That's right, asshole. Special Agent. Now tell me what the fuck you're doing here before I arrest you."

"If you want to continue being 'Special Agent' Leon, I suggest you sit down, please," Alvarez said. "Does the Bureau know about your gambling problem?"

Leon stopped in his tracks as Alvarez tossed a set of large photo prints on the table in front of him. "Look familiar?" Alvarez asked.

Leon picked up the pictures and studied them. They were pictures of him sitting in the stands at the track.

"So what?" Leon asked indignantly. "Are you trying to blackmail me? Going to the track isn't illegal."

Alvarez said nothing as he tossed two more pictures on the table. In them, Leon was giving cash to Rubio.

"So tell on me, I don't fucking care. They'll slap me on the wrist and make me get counseling. Big deal." Leon was playing it off pretty well. Alvarez had to give it to him.

"I understand," Alvarez said as he tossed two more pictures on the table. This time, the pictures were black and white and of him with a naked woman on top. "That doesn't look like your wife."

"I'm sure that bitch is cheating on me anyway, and

you can't prove this is illegal," Leon replied, tossing the pictures back at Alvarez. "Now if you'll get the fuck out of here, I've got an appointment."

Alvarez smiled as Leon mentioned his cheating wife. *If he only knew.*

"About that gambling thing," Alvarez said, pulling a piece of paper out of his pocket. "Ten thousand dollars in the hole this month. Ten thousand last month. Five thousand dollar debt to Juan Rubio at 60% interest. Twenty one hundred dollars left to your name. I don't think Mr. Rubio or his associates will accept Gamblers Anonymous as payment, Agent Leon."

Leon stumbled back and sat back down on the couch. "Who are you? What do you want?"

"My name is Victor," Alvarez responded. "And I would like to make all your problems go away."

"I'm listening," Leon said, cautiously leaning forward.

Alvarez tossed a black duffle bag to Leon's feet. He waited as Leon unzipped the top and pulled out a stack of neatly packaged $100 bills.

"There's one hundred thousand dollars in cash in that bag, Agent Leon," Alvarez said as he sat back and crossed his legs. "You can use that to pay off your debt to Mr. Rubio. After that, you are done with that track. You will then receive ten thousand dollars per month. All cash, of course."

"In exchange for what? Why would you do this?" Leon asked, thumbing through the bills.

"Friendship."

"Friendship?"

Alvarez stood and extended his hand to Leon. "I would like your friendship, Special Agent. That is all."

Leon stared at the outstretched hand. He considered it for a moment, and then grabbed Victor's hand, shaking it as he stood. Alvarez seemed to tower over the short little man.

"To friendship," Leon said with a crooked smile.

"You've made the right choice," Alvarez responded, patting Leon on the shoulder with his free hand.

Cal "Spectre" Martin

First Impressions

Warning Area 465
Atlantic Ocean
15 September 2007

"Gator 11 is ready."

"Gator 12 is ready," he replied as he wiggled his fingers around the throttle and sidestick of his F-16. He was fixated on his flight lead, a mile and a half down his wingline directly to his right.

"Gators, check forty five right."

First Lieutenant Cal Martin's heart was racing as he maneuvered his F-16 into position behind his flight lead. It was his first flight with his new squadron, and he wanted to make a good impression. A Reservist, Martin was the first Gator hired off the street to make it through the training pipeline in over ten years. Aside from the active duty pilots assigned to the 39th Fighter Squadron, Martin was the most inexperienced pilot in a squadron full of thousand plus hour combat veterans.

"One point nine," Martin called over the radio as he took a radar lock. They were doing an Offensive 9K perch setup as part of his first Mission Qualification

Training upgrade flight. His flight lead would give him the initial advantage and Martin's job was to maneuver his F-16 from a mile and a half behind his flight lead into a position to get a guns kill.

His flight lead reversed the direction of the turn to set up the appropriate angle between the two fighters for Martin. With perch setups, Martin had been taught that the initial parameters were the most important. It was essential for both aircraft to be at the same airspeed, altitude, and angle off tail to ensure the right sight picture for follow on maneuvering. It was part of a building block approach to move from canned, controlled setups to more dynamic high aspect dogfighting where the student could then apply the sight pictures he had seen before.

"One point eight," Martin said as he watched the range count down in his Head Up Display. Martin was nervous. He was flying with the squadron's Weapons Officer, Major "Magic" Manny. A good gradesheet from Magic would set the tone for the rest of his Mission Qualification Upgrade Training. A busted flight or "Below Average" grade would set him up for more scrutiny from other Instructor Pilots. It was time to show off what he had learned in the F-16 Basic Course at Luke AFB.

"One point seven." He wiggled his fingers and toes, trying to relax and concentrate on keeping his flight lead's F-16 under the boresight cross in the HUD. At a range of a mile and a half, he was starting the fight outside the imaginary "turn circle" the turning adversary's aircraft traced across the sky. He would have to roll out, recognize the turn circle entry cues he had been taught, and then successfully align with the adversary aircraft's flight path without over or undershooting. Enter too early, and his attacker would create too many angles for him to solve and eventually neutralize him. Enter too late, and he would go from offensive to neutral or even defensive as the attacker reversed.

"One point six."

"Fight's on!" Martin said as the range reached 1.5nm in the HUD.

Martin rolled wings level and selected full afterburner as he watched Magic's F-16 enter its defensive break turn and pop out flares. Martin drove straight ahead as he looked for his turn circle entry cues — at first Magic's jet would look like it was just rotating in space, and then it would suddenly go from rotational to translational motion as it zipped past his canopy. Just before that, his instructors had told him, he needed to be rolling and pulling while starting his Anti-G Straining Maneuver.

As Martin neared that point, he crosschecked his airspeed. He was going much faster than he wanted to. He had flown heavier F-16 Block 42s with smaller engines in school, but this Block 30 F-16 was a hotrod. Its thrust to weight ratio easily exceeded 1:1 in its current configuration, and the big General Electric engine had no trouble accelerating the slick F-16 through 500 knots – *way too fast.*

Martin tried cycling the throttle from full afterburner back to military power, but it was too late. He had to start his turn in that instant or he'd fly right out the back of Magic's turn circle and he'd end up defensive. Martin took a deep breath as he prepared for the onset of G-forces and squeezed his abs and legs.

As Martin started his pull, the jet stabilized in the turn at a sustained 9G pull. He was now feeling the force of nine times his bodyweight pressing against him, pulling the blood from his brain into his feet as his G-suit inflated against his legs and torso. Martin strained against the G-forces as he took short breaths every three seconds. If he exhaled completely, he wouldn't be able to get air back in his lungs, and would eventually be starved of oxygen. He strained as hard as he could as the G-forces caused his vision to tunnel slightly.

Magic reoriented from slightly nose low to a more oblique turn as Martin continued his pursuit. Martin tried to maintain his position of advantage as Magic spiraled toward the crystal blue Atlantic Ocean below them in an attempt to shrink his turn circle and keep Martin from being able to employ weapons.

As Magic neared their training floor of ten thousand feet, Martin maintained an altitude advantage, waiting for Magic's turn circle to open back up as he could no longer go downhill, increasing his turn radius. Once Martin had his attack cues, he traded his altitude advantage and saddled in behind Magic. As they transitioned to the floor, the G-forces subsided and Martin focused on his gun employment.

Martin pulled his nose around to put the computed gun pipper on Magic. Seeing that Martin was in a gun employment zone, Manny immediately rolled into a tuck under jink, forcing Martin to reposition before he could saddle in and shoot. As Magic rolled out, Martin squeezed the trigger and watched as the imaginary bullets went through the fuselage of Magic's aircraft.

"Gator 12, kill Viper left hand turn," Martin said over their fight frequency.

"Copy kill, Gators knock it off, Gator 11 knock it off," Magic replied, signaling that the set was over.

"Gator 12, knock it off," Martin responded as he repositioned his aircraft in a loose formation behind Magic.

As they climbed back up to their starting altitude for the next set, Magic did a fuel check over the radio and set them up for another fight.

"Not too bad," Magic said, offering a real time assessment of the previous set, "just a little slow to get to a guns track, and a slightly late turn circle entry."

"2," Martin replied sharply. It was not a discussion. Wingman were expected to keep their mouths shut and ears open.

"You're going to want to get the quickest kill possible, in case the bandit's buddies are in the area," Magic continued.

"2!"

"Let's try it again, any questions?" Magic asked as he gave Martin the visual signal to move out to a tactical formation.

"Negative," Martin replied. He was determined to make it right. He had to show Magic that he could get the quick kill. *He wouldn't screw it up this time.*

Once they reached the appropriate altitude, they each called ready as before and Magic called the check turn. Magic reversed his turn as Martin started calling down ranges.

"Fight's on!" Martin called as he reached a mile and a half. He lit the afterburner and rolled out as he drove toward Magic's turn circle, but this time he started a shallow climb and checked away to slow his acceleration.

The sight picture was just different. As Magic continued his break turn, Martin rolled into a descending turn and sliced back toward him. The visual cues were different from what he was expecting, but almost immediately he saw what he thought to be attack cues – Magic's airplane appeared to be nearly as long as it was wide.

Martin continued to pull Magic's F-16 toward his HUD. It was going to be a high aspect gun shot. He had one chance to get it right before Magic could reverse, but with the higher aspect angle, Martin had more of Magic's aircraft available to shoot.

Martin pulled back on the sidestick with everything he had and tried to stabilize Magic in the HUD. He squeezed the trigger, raking the pipper through Magic's jet as it screamed by him. Once he let off the trigger, he tried to pull up to maintain his advantage, but Magic had already capitalized and the two were now side-by-side and jockeying for position.

"Gator knock it off, Gator 11 knock it off," Magic said over the radio.

"Gator 12 knock it off," Martin echoed.

"We can talk about that one on the ground, let's move on to the next set," Magic said after confirming their fuel state. Martin's face felt flush. He wasn't sure if he had gotten enough of a stable track to count as a kill, so he hadn't called it. Either way, he was afraid Magic now thought he was terrible for not maintaining the offensive. So much for making a good first impression.

******

"Questions on the brief?" Magic asked as he stood in front of the white board in the small briefing room.

"None," Martin responded.

"Questions on the motherhood?" Magic asked, referring to the administrative portion of the mission getting to and from the airspace to fight.

"No, sir," Martin replied. He was still thinking about the first two sets. He had done fine in the subsequent short-range 6000' and 3000' sets, but he feared that the first two would be enough to give him his first bust as a Gator. *Not a good way to shine as a new wingman.*

Magic laughed and said, "Don't call me 'Sir.' This is a Reserve squadron, we're all bros here."

"Yes, sir," Martin replied. "Dammit, sorry!"

"Ok, let's take a look at the tapes," Magic said as he pulled up the computer debriefing program. The "tapes" had long since been replaced by Digital Video Recorders, but years later, people were still calling them tapes.

As they watched the first set, Magic paused the DVR as he watched Martin accelerate toward the turn circle. "You see your airspeed? You're way too fast here. That's why it takes so long. You're not getting a good rate and your turn circle is huge."

Martin nodded and took notes as Magic hit PLAY again.

"And that's why you're sustaining 9Gs for so long. That had to hurt," Magic said, wincing.

Martin looked at his forearms. The tiny ruptured capillaries, or "G-easles" as they were known, that peppered his arm were evidence of that.

They continued watching the fight as Magic gave Martin pointers on how to fix it properly.

"Any questions on that set?" Magic asked after confirming that Martin's guns track was valid and sufficient to call a kill.

"None."

"Ok, let's watch the second one," Magic said with a frown. He advanced the DVR to the start of the second set.

"Your parameters look good at the start, but why the climb?" Magic said as he paused the DVR. The HUD showed Martin ten degrees nose high.

"I was afraid to get fast again, I wasn't really thinking," Martin replied flatly. He didn't want to make excuses. Good wingman didn't make excuses or try to explain what they were thinking.

"Copy. Try modulating the throttle or using speed brakes next time," Magic said as he hit PLAY again.

Magic let the DVR play through as Martin went from nose high to slicing back down toward Magic's jet. As Martin pulled Magic's jet into the HUD, Magic stopped the DVR.

"Straight to the HUD, huh? Did you have your attack cues met?" Magic asked.

Martin shook his head without saying anything. It looked right in the air, but he couldn't say that. The book answer was that he did not have the appropriate cues to execute an attack. The cues were specific and definable. Gut feelings were not.

"This will lead to the ninety-degree off overshoot and subsequent reversal," Magic said as he hit PLAY again.

They watched in silence as Martin stabilized Magic's aircraft in the HUD and the display showed the simulated bullets hitting Magic's aircraft.

"Wait, you tried to shoot here?" Magic said, pausing the footage and rewinding.

Martin said nothing as Magic hit the rewind button. He stopped as the green dots simulating bullets started to hit his fuselage, and then started advancing the footage frame by frame to count bullets.

As he reached twenty-five, he stopped the DVR, staring at it. Martin had more than exceeded the required number of frames to call a kill.

"You gunned me off the perch in a 9K set," Magic said, stunned. "*Wow*, kid."

Martin looked up from his notes. He had been wincing as Magic slowly went through the gunshot. He knew that this was a pretty big make or break moment for him.

"I've only known a few people that could pull that off," Magic said, "and none of them were brand new lieutenants."

Martin tried not to smile as he realized the compliment. It was a pretty big deal to hear that from the squadron Weapons Officer.

"Were you trying to do that?" Magic asked. "Or was it luck?"

"I guess it was just luck," Martin said humbly. "I just did what looked right."

Magic considered the statement for a moment, creating an uncomfortable silence as he seemed to look Martin up and down.

"Well, luck or not, it was a good shot. But I wouldn't make a habit of it. We teach lag BFM for a reason. We want results you can replicate over and over, not lucky shots. This is a bit too aggressive. If you miss a shot like this in combat, you're dead."

Martin nodded.

After asking if Martin had any further questions, he advanced to the next set. They debriefed the final four shorter-range sets the same as the first two, and then Magic sat down across the debriefing table from Martin after recapping their objectives.

"Overall, I'd say you did a good job today. Definitely above average," Magic said leaning back in the chair.

Martin exhaled as the words "Above Average" hung in the air. He had been worried during the entire debrief that he might have to refly the flight. He definitely wasn't expecting such praise.

"You've got good hands and a good attitude. I saw your pilot training gradebooks. You've done well. You might be a little too aggressive, and that could get you in trouble, but I can work with aggressive. It's way easier to throttle someone back than try to make them more aggressive."

Martin nodded sheepishly. He didn't know how to respond to such high praise

"Has the boss talked to you yet?"

"About what?" Martin asked, tilting his head to the side.

Magic looked at his watch and said, "About why it's six o'clock and there's no fucking popcorn yet."

Martin's faced reddened. As the most junior guy in the squadron, his additional duty was to keep the squadron bar cleaned and stocked with beer and snacks, and ensure fresh jalapeno popcorn was ready every evening.

"No excuse," Martin said stoically.

"I'm just giving you shit!" Magic busted out laughing. "I meant about the F-22 thing."

Martin gave him a confused look.

"I guess not. Well, don't be surprised if the boss talks to you about it. I know you just got here and everything, but the Reserves are standing up their F-22 associate program and looking for a young wingman with good hands to be the first young Reserve guy in the community. Think you might be interested?"

"Hell yes!" Martin replied. His stoic demeanor was replaced by a childish enthusiasm. He couldn't contain himself.

"Keep doing what you're doing and you might just be that guy," Magic replied.

Martin was grinning ear to ear. *This squadron was awesome.* He couldn't wait for his next flight.

"Now go make some popcorn!" Magic barked.

Sean Baxter

The Truth is in the Details

Hwy 315
West of Clayton, Texas
8 August 2010
0130L

Trooper Sean Baxter had only been working nights for two weeks, but he hated it. As he droned down the empty four lane county highway, he cursed himself for volunteering to work the county roads. Weeknights in East Texas were usually pretty boring. No one stayed out past midnight on weekdays, and when they did, they were usually just drunken rednecks that were impossible to deal with. Not that tasing drunken rednecks wasn't fun, but he hoped it wouldn't be the highlight of his career.

Sean Baxter had joined the Texas State Troopers to become a Texas Ranger. Son of a Secret Service Agent killed in the line of duty, Baxter had grown up with the dream of continuing the family business. But with budget cutbacks and the civilian sector struggling under a recession when he graduated college two years prior, the Secret Service just wasn't hiring.

Despite having moved around following his dad's assignments most of his young life, Baxter considered himself a Texan. So it was only natural that he'd want to become a Texas Ranger when the Feds weren't hiring, and since the Rangers required the rank of Trooper II with Department of Public Safety State Troopers, Baxter's only option was to start as a Trooper.

And so he found himself at fifty-five miles per hour on a desolate county road in the wee hours of the morning on a hot August night. It wasn't the action-packed job of protecting the President or chasing down counterfeiters he had hoped for. Instead, he was relegated to handing out speeding tickets and beating down drunks. Aside from the night transition, it was still law enforcement and he still loved it. Protecting and serving was his calling.

As Baxter continued down the featureless highway in his standard-issue black and white Crown Victoria, another sedan pulled out in front of him off a dirt road and accelerated. Baxter tapped the brakes to avoid overrunning the car and perked up. *Another drunk?*

Baxter paced the car at a safe distance. It wasn't swerving or driving recklessly. His left taillight was out, but other than that, the driver hadn't committed any major violations. The car just appeared to be out later than everyone else.

Baxter's father was killed when Baxter was a young teen, but he had always talked to him about being a good investigator. "The truth is always in the details," he had said. His dad told him countless stories of doing protection details or doing investigations in which the tiniest detail had been the difference between a case going cold and an arrest and conviction being made. The Academy had honed those skills, and for the time being, the details were bothering him. *What was a car doing out here at this hour with a busted tail light?*

Baxter sped up to within a car length of the sedan. It was a newer Chevy Malibu. The driver's side taillight wasn't just out. *It was completely missing.* Baxter ran the plate through his laptop. The car and registered owner were clean- no arrest warrants or reports of being stolen. Baxter decided to pull the car over anyway.

He turned on his light bar and called in the stop to dispatch. The driver put his turn signal on and pulled over to the side of the road uneventfully. Baxter composed himself and turned on the spotlight on his driver's door. He grabbed his Trooper hat and stepped out of the car.

The Malibu's driver side door swung open and a man started to exit. Baxter's hand immediately went to his sidearm, a Glock 21 chambered in .45ACP.

"Sir, please remain in your vehicle," Baxter ordered from behind his own door. The hair on the back of his neck was now standing up.

The man complied, swung his leg back into the vehicle, and closed the door. He lowered his window and put his hands on the steering wheel. Baxter cautiously approached, still guarding his Glock with his right hand and holding a flashlight with his left. As he approached the rear quarter panel, he could see the tail light wiring hanging loosely. The bulb and taillight assembly were missing completely.

Baxter approached the window cautiously. He had seen far too many training videos of Troopers getting shot in situations like these. He refused to lower his guard.

"Sir, do you know why I stopped you?" Baxter asked as he reached the window. The man looked up at him as Baxter shined his light into the car. He looked nervous. His hands were fidgeting while holding the steering wheel. "Your left taillight is out."

The man didn't respond.

"Sir, I'm going to need you to turn off the vehicle and give me your license, registration, and proof of insurance," Baxter said, still standing sideways, ready to draw if necessary.

The man slowly reached for the glove compartment. He opened it, and a flood of papers fell out. Baxter watched as the man fished through them and found his registration and proof of insurance. He handed them to Baxter, along with his ID. Baxter studied the ID for a moment, watching for a reaction out of the corner of his eye. The man was shifty. He had not said a word yet, but his eyes kept darting from the front to Baxter and then to the Baxter's cruiser.

"Sir, please step out of the vehicle," Baxter said as he stepped away from the door.

"Is there something wrong officer?" the man finally asked. His voice was low and hoarse.

"No sir, I just need you to stand back at the rear of the vehicle while I run your information. It's standard procedure," Baxter replied.

The man hesitated for a minute and then slowly opened the door and got out. He was an older man. His license showed him to be 55, but he looked like he was easily in his late sixties. He was balding, with patches of hair on the sides. He was wearing a white t-shirt and jean shorts with sandals. He looked like he hadn't shaved in a few days.

Baxter ushered him to the rear of the vehicle and told him to wait. Baxter got in his cruiser and called in the information. He watched the man as he waited for the results. *The truth is always in the details.* The man stood there, arms folded. His body language was fairly benign, but his eyes told another story. He kept looking at the trunk and looking back at Baxter. Baxter called it in and asked to have the county Sheriff's K-9 unit on standby for backup. The guy could have easily been moving drugs this late at night.

Baxter decided to write him a warning for the taillight. He was more interested in what the guy was so nervous about. After he finished writing, he approached the man cautiously.

"Mr. Jenkins," Baxter said, reading the man's license, "I'm going to issue you a warning for your busted tail light. You're going to need to get that fixed as soon as possible."

The man didn't look at Baxter. His gaze was now shifting between the trunk and the asphalt.

"Is there something wrong, Mr. Jenkins?" Baxter asked.

"No," the man mumbled, still staring at the ground.

"Where are you headed tonight?"

The man mumbled something unintelligible.

"I'm sorry?" Baxter asked.

The man repeated himself.

"Sir, have you been drinking?" Baxter asked. He had already been watching him for signs of alcohol use. He didn't have it on his breath, and his motor skills and eyes did not seem to indicate alcohol use.

The man's eyes widened as he looked up at Baxter. "No, no, no, no, no sir!"

"Do I have your permission to search your vehicle?"

The man stood there, staring at Baxter like a deer caught in headlights. The man glanced back at Baxter one last time. Baxter instantly recognized what was about to happen. The man felt cornered, and his fight or flight instinct had just kicked in. The man took off running toward the nearby field. Baxter gave chase as he radioed in for backup.

The man may have looked ten years older than he was, but he ran like a man twenty years younger. Weighted down by his vest and gear, it took Baxter longer than he would later admit to catch the man thirty years his senior, but within seconds, he had the man pinned to the ground and cuffed.

"Why are you running, Mr. Jenkins?" Baxter asked as held the man down.

"They're so beautiful, but I could only keep one," the man said as he started sobbing.

"Who's beautiful? What are you talking about?" Baxter demanded as he pulled the man to his feet out of the field.

"She's my little angel," the man said between sobs.

"Who is?" Baxter shoved the man toward his cruiser. Once they reached the rear quarter panel, he searched him for weapons or drugs, pulling out a knife, some zip ties, and a key to a padlock. He opened the rear door of his cruiser and put the man inside. He was crying uncontrollably now.

With the man secured, Baxter went back to the Malibu. He searched the front seats. There were fast food bags and wrappers everywhere. He looked through the backseat, but only found little girls' clothing and empty grocery bags.

Baxter went back to the front and pulled the trunk release. His adrenaline spiked as he reached the back and open the trunk. There lay a little girl, her hands bound by zip ties and her mouth gagged. She was unconscious. Baxter keyed his radio requesting medical support as he picked up the little girl out of the trunk. Her blond hair was dirty and her clothes torn. Her breathing was shallow.

Baxter carried her toward his cruiser as the first

Sheriff's Deputy cruiser arrived on scene. The deputy got out of his cruiser and went straight for his trunk, pulling out a blanket for the little girl and opening the back door for Baxter to lay her down. The girl came to as Baxter searched her for any wounds or bleeding.

"Where... Where am I?" she croaked. She couldn't be older than 6 or 7, Baxter guessed.

"My name is Sean, and I'm a police officer, you're safe, now," Baxter said reassuringly. "What's your name, sweetie?"

"Kayla," the girl said timidly.

"Well, Kayla, it's nice to meet you, everything is going to be ok," Baxter said as he held the little girl's hands. She had dirt under her fingernails and all over her hands.

"Where's Abigail? Where is she?!" the girl suddenly screamed.

"You're ok. You're safe now. Who is Abigail?" Baxter asked, trying to calm the girl.

"She's my sister," the girl replied, wiping a tear from her eyes.

"Was she with you? Can you tell me what happened?" Baxter responded. He was squatting down next to the girl as he tried to calm her down.

"That man took her," she said flatly, as she gazed off into the distance.

Baxter turned as a deputy tapped him on the shoulder. They stepped away to the rear of the cruiser.

"That's one of the Harris girls," he said. "Went

missing yesterday. Twins. Parents said they were out playing in the woods and didn't come home."

An ambulance arrived as Baxter walked back to talk to the little girl.

"Kayla, can you tell me where you were?" Baxter asked. He was trying to piece together the puzzle. The man had mentioned only being able to take one of the girls and little Kayla was panicked about her sister. He hoped he could get some information to find the missing twin.

"I don't know," she began, "it was so dark. I kicked until there was light, but it didn't stop."

Baxter thought back to the taillight. The little girl must have kicked it out while they were driving.

"Did you hear anything? Anything at all?" Baxter prodded.

"Moo!" the girl said, looking up at Baxter.

"Moo?"

"I heard moo cows," the girl replied.

"Did you hear anything else?"

"Where's Abby? I want my mommy," the girl said as she started to cry.

"We'll find her," Baxter assured the little girl. He stepped back as the paramedics walked up to look the girl over. Baxter walked back to where the deputies were standing, discussing the missing girl.

"We'll transfer Jenkins to lock-up," the deputy said.

"The other little girl is still missing," Baxter replied with a frown. He knew time might have already run out.

There was no telling what that psychopath had done to little Abigail Harris.

"They live in the next county over," the deputy responded. "He could have taken them anywhere."

Baxter thought about it for a moment. Without saying a word, he walked up to his cruiser and opened the back door. "Get out," he said as he grabbed Jenkins' arm and pulled him out of the car. Jenkins reluctantly complied, stumbling as he was pulled out of the car.

"Where's the other girl?" Baxter asked.

"She's an angel now," the man responded. He was still sobbing.

"You son of a bitch, what did you do to her?" Baxter demanded as he slammed the man against the cruiser.

"She's sleeping now," the man responded. Baxter grabbed the man and shoved him toward the other deputy. The deputy caught him as he nearly tripped and fell.

Baxter walked back to the man's car. The trunk was still open. He looked inside, seeing dirt and dust everywhere. It looked like red dirt or clay.

"Deputy!" Baxter said, motioning to the Sheriff's Deputy he had been talking to.

"What's up?" the deputy asked as he finished helping the other deputy stuff Jenkins in his cruiser.

"This guy pulled onto the highway off a dirt road about a mile that way," he said, pointing past the cruisers and ambulance.

"Yeah?"

"Do you know what's down that road?"

"Mostly pastures, a farm, and a pond, I think," the deputy replied.

"Get in your car and follow me!" Baxter said as he sprinted toward his cruiser. The confused deputy hesitated and then took off toward his car as Baxter slammed his door shut. He made a u-turn and floored it, heading toward the road the man had pulled out from as the Crown Vic's V8 engine screamed.

As Baxter reached the road, he made a left, slowing as his wheels hit the packed gravel. He turned on his spotlight and looked out. There were fields with barbed wire fences on either side. The Sheriff's Deputy finally caught up behind him and also began searching with his spotlight. Baxter kept driving slowly. He didn't really know what he was looking for exactly, but he knew he'd recognize it if he saw it. *The truth was in the details.*

After a half mile, the road came to a T-intersection with another gravel road. Baxter stopped and got out of his car. He walked into the middle of the intersecting road with his flashlight. To his left, it looked like there was a gate that led to more field. The path to his right seemed to go on for another mile or so. The deputy got out and approached Baxter as he stood contemplating which way to go.

"Where does that road lead?" Baxter asked, pointing to his right down the dark gravel road.

"More farms, woods, and back out to the highway,"

the deputy replied.

Baxter considered it for a second. As he stared at the metal gate, it hit him. He pulled out the key he'd taken from Jenkins during the pat down.

"Worth a shot," Baxter said as he walked back to his car.

The two drove up to the metal gate. Baxter got out and used his flashlight to look around. The metal gate gave way to a grassy path that was freshly laid down. Someone had driven over it recently. Baxter decided to try the key. As he twisted it, the padlock clicked open and he pulled the iron chain away from the metal gate.

"Winner," Baxter said as he pushed the gate open. Baxter and the deputy walked down the path, their flashlights darting about as they looked for clues. They stopped in their tracks as they heard a rustle. Both men drew their weapons, only to realize it was a cow. There were three of them grazing right by the fence line. The path they were on ran parallel to the northern fence line of the field. *The cow!* They were on the right track.

Baxter and the deputy followed the vehicle tracks. The full moon nearly turned night into day, lighting up the small pond and cabin in the distance. As Baxter and the deputy approached, they looked for signs of life, but it was completely vacant.

"Now what?" the deputy asked as they reached the edge of the pond.

"We go in," Baxter said as he held up the key. "Probable cause."

The two cautiously approached the cabin. It was small and it looked like it had been there for decades. The wood appeared to be rotting. Baxter tried the door handle. It was unlocked. He pushed the door open carefully, crossing his gun and over his flashlight as he swept the room.

There was a bed in the corner and a small stove, but otherwise it was barren. As Baxter swept the room with the flashlight, he could see streaks of blood on the floor and sheets. The two moved forward, toward the back door.

"Jesus," the deputy said. "You think this is where he did…whatever it is he did?"

"I don't know," Baxter said as he approached the back door. "Better call it in."

The deputy radioed to dispatch as Baxter opened the back door. The door opened up to another side of the pond. There was a large pine tree surrounded by dirt. Baxter turned to his right and noticed a shovel leaning against side of the cabin. He picked it up. It still had dirt around the edges. He picked off a piece of dried dirt with his fingers.

"Red dirt," he said to himself as he examined the dirt. He remembered the trunk. There had been red dirt everywhere. Baxter frantically shined his flashlight around the small pond as he approached the lone tree.

"Back up is on the way," the deputy said as he joined Baxter.

"Look for fresh dirt," Baxter said as he held up his

fingers. "Someone has been digging."

The two walked around the pond, searching for signs of freshly moved earth. Baxter froze as his flashlight glanced across a clump of dirt near the water's edge. *Was that it?* Baxter sprinted for the shovel. He picked it up off the ground and ran back to where he had seen the clump of dirt. It looked as if Jenkins had tried to pack it down, but had done a poor job. He started to dig. The deputy searched the outside of the cabin and found another shovel.

The two immediately started digging, hitting something solid only minutes later. "Found something!" Baxter yelled. His once-neatly-pressed uniform was completely covered in dirt and drenched in sweat. They desperately continued digging, finally revealing a small wooden box. Once it was exposed enough, Baxter used the shovel as leverage to pry the box open. It had been nailed shut.

"Jesus Christ," Baxter said as he pulled the wooden top off. There he saw a small girl, curled in the fetal position. Her mouth was gagged and her hands had been zip-tied together. She was pale and dirty, wearing only her underwear. The deputy stepped back in horror.

Baxter knelt down next to the little girl. It was horrific seeing the little girl like that. *That sick son of a bitch*, he thought. He reached down and touched her arm. It was cool and clammy. He moved up to her neck and started to check her pulse.

"This is sick," the deputy said. "How could anyone

do this? There's no way she's alive."

Baxter ignored him. He moved his two fingers to the side of her neck. He felt nothing. Baxter closed his eyes and sighed. Suddenly he felt what he thought to be a pulse. It was weak and thready, but he felt something. He swapped hands, thinking he was willing himself to believe she was still alive.

"She has a pulse!" Baxter screamed. "Help me get her out!"

Baxter picked up the small girl and pulled her to the side of the shallow grave. She had to get to a hospital soon. She was barely breathing, but she was alive.

"I'll call it in!" the deputy said.

"She doesn't have time!" Baxter said as he picked up the little girl and started running toward his cruiser. The girl couldn't have weighed more than sixty pounds, but Baxter's legs were burning as he tried to run, carrying her to his car. The deputy sprinted ahead, opening the back door of Baxter's cruiser and getting in his own car to get out of the way. Baxter laid the small girl down on the back seat and covered her with a blanket. He got in his still running cruiser and floored it in reverse, kicking up rocks and gravel as he turned around.

As they reached the highway, the two police cars stormed down the empty road, both with lights and siren blaring. The town of Clayton was only a few miles down the road, but the little girl needed every second she could get. A lone car pulled over to the side of the road as the two cruisers rocketed by. Baxter radioed ahead to have the ER ready upon his arrival.

The trauma team was waiting as Baxter rounded the corner behind the deputy's car into the ER loading bay. They loaded the girl onto a gurney and put her on 100% oxygen immediately as they wheeled her into the Emergency Room. Baxter watched as they worked. The girl was fading fast, but still alive. He couldn't believe it. She had been buried alive in a shallow grave. It was only luck that he had found her. Luck and the nagging voice of his father to always pay attention to the details.

Joe Carpenter

Hawg Highway

Bamiyan Charikar Highway
Bamiyan Province, Afghanistan
July 2013 1800L

The six-vehicle convoy drove steadily down the
newly paved valley highway. The four MRAPs and two
HUMVEEs were seemingly the only vehicles within
miles as the mountain peaks on either side cast their
shadows onto the hot asphalt, shielding them from the
hot desert sun they had been exposed to all day.

The dull droning of the all-terrain tires on the barely
paved asphalt was almost relaxing to Tech Sgt Joe
Carpenter. If it weren't for the fifty pounds of gear and
lack of airflow through the up-armored HUMVEE he
was riding shotgun in, it might have made for a nice
environment to take a nap.

A nap sounded great to Carpenter as he stared
listlessly at the MRAP in the convoy ahead of them. He
had gone outside the wire early that morning with an
International Security Assistance Force composed
mostly of U.S. Army and a few Afghan National Army
soldiers. They had spent most of the day in the Bamiyan

Province, assisting the local police with security and giving the ANA soldiers more on-the-job training before the upcoming troop drawdown.

It was Carpenter's second time in Afghanistan, although it was his first in an Air Force uniform. He had hiked those same mountain peaks as an Army Ranger six years prior, going door to door to find and capture or kill Taliban fighters. The irony that he was back in the same part of the country with the Army had not escaped him.

"I fucking hate this time of day," SSGT Gomez said, breaking the silence. Gomez was a native Texan who had been in the Army since he was just out of high school. He had told Carpenter that it was the only thing keeping him off the streets of El Paso and gangs.

"At least we're heading back," Carpenter offered. "It's only another hour or so to Bagram."

"I don't care about being out. I love being out. It's this shadow valley shit I hate. It's too bright for NVGs, but there are too many fucking shadows out there to see assholes sneaking across ridges. We're just targets on this highway. It's fucking stupid," Gomez replied. They were the only two in the vehicle, driving closely behind the lead MRAP- the Army's Mine-Resistant Ambush Protected armored fighting vehicle designed to withstand IED attacks and ambushes.

"I hear ya man. But it's been pretty quiet out here the last four months," Carpenter replied, shrugging under his body armor.

"Yeah, fucking thanks! Make my point for me! *Too* fucking quiet!" Gomez responded.

Carpenter sighed. He remembered that feeling from his time in the Army. This was his first real deployment outside the wire since those days, having spent most of his deployed time in the Air Force within the confines of Baghdad International Airport and the Green Zone in Iraq.

He had been an Air Force Tactical Air Control Party qualified as a Joint Terminal Attack Controller for three years after going Green to Blue in search of a more aviation-oriented career. Unable to fly because of a color vision test, he landed right back with the Army, as an embedded Air Force JTAC.

Doing perhaps one of the most physically demanding jobs in the Air Force, JTACs were frontline battlefield airmen. They were embedded with ground forces to advise the ground commander on Air Force air power capabilities, and in the heat of battle, to control aircraft during close air support scenarios. Of course, it was just Carpenter's luck that he'd get out of the Army just to go back in a different uniform, but he didn't mind, he was at the tip of the spear and he loved it.

To Carpenter, though, the best thing about working for Mother Blue was the toys. He knew the Army had the same technology and capabilities, but in the Air Force, he always seemed to have the latest and greatest at his fingertips.

"Movement up ahead, south ridge line," a voice said

over their discrete convoy communications frequency.

"See? No good can come of this," Gomez said as he strained to look around the MRAP in front of them for the movement that had just been called out.

Carpenter pulled a set of binoculars from his backpack and looked out onto the ridge. He scanned for any movement or activity as they continued down the highway.

"I don't see any-" Carpenter was interrupted by the blast. The MRAP in front of them seemed to be lifted up and thrown back to the ground as Gomez swerved the HUMVEE to avoid hitting it. It skidded to a stop in the ditch paralleling the road as it showered the road with sparks and dust.

"IED! We're hit! Sandman 11 is hit!" the driver of the lead vehicle said over radio.

"Keep moving!" another voice said over the radio. To Carpenter, it sounded like the Convoy Commander. He had been riding with Carpenter and Gomez all day, but at the last village had swapped to the MRAP serving as a gun truck behind them.

"Unable sir! 11 has lost steering!" the lead vehicle commander replied.

"Holy shit!" Gomez said as they pulled up next to the damaged MRAP that was now resting nose first in the ditch. "That fucking thing blew off a wheel!"

Carpenter instinctively ducked as rounds started peppering the armor of their HUMVEE.

"Ambush!" Gomez yelled over the radio. The

mounted gun on the disabled MRAP came alive as it sent rounds toward the ridgeline

"All players, blocking positions, set up a perimeter around Sandman 11," the Convoy Commander directed.

"I'll get on that fifty," Carpenter said as he slid by Gomez toward the roof-mounted .50 caliber machine gun.

Carpenter climbed into the gunner's seat and checked the .50. He was surrounded on all sides by bulletproof panels, but he had a much better view than he'd had inside the HUMVEE. He tried to pinpoint the direction of fire as the three other MRAPs and HUMVEE moved into position around the damaged lead MRAP.

"Mortars! Incoming!" Carpenter heard over the radio as the bullets continued plinking against the driver's side of the HUMVEE. Carpenter ducked down as the first mortar hit. It landed in the dirt, just a few meters off the road near the downed MRAP. It shot up dirt and debris in a cloud of dust as it hit with a loud explosion.

Carpenter rotated the turret and started firing in the direction of the incoming fire, hoping to lay down suppressive fire as the .50 cal roared to life. He picked up movement out of the corner of his eye and turned. He immediately found one of the enemy fighters on one knee sporadically firing his AK-47. Carpenter turned and fired, ripping the man to shreds with his large caliber machine gun.

As Carpenter continued to fire in the vicinity of the last fighter, he saw a figure approach as men from the MRAPs dismounted. The man was short, even with boots and a helmet, but he walked as if he were seven feet tall and bulletproof. Despite the bullets zipping by and mortars at random intervals, he seemed completely unaffected as he calmly walked to Carpenter's HUMVEE and climbed in.

"Gomez, relieve Carpenter on that fifty," he barked. "Carpenter, get your ass down here, we need air support." It was Major Hilton, the no-nonsense convoy commander who had been riding with them most of the day until the trip back to Bagram.

Carpenter and Gomez swapped positions and Carpenter went to work with his gear. He pulled out his Harris PRC-117F and powered it up. The dismounted radio, called a manpack, served as a multi-band, multimode radio that covered the gamut of waveforms. Frequencies covered included VHF, UHF, and UHF SATCOM radio. The unit was also compatible with the Single Channel Ground and Airborne Radio System, an Army system. It served as a lifeline for any JTAC to support assets in the air.

"Son, you need to call this in. We've got a disabled MRAP and I estimate approximately one hundred fighters approaching from two separate locations. We're going to need CAS birds and ISR to make sure the rest of the route is clear, understand?"

Carpenter nodded as he wrote down the situation

report in the appropriate format. He needed to call in to the FIRES desk to request the Close Air Support and Intelligence, Surveillance, and Reconnaissance tasking orders. With the air order of battle he had seen earlier in the day, he was pretty sure he could at least get a Predator drone on station to scan the route fairly quickly, but he wasn't sure what assets would be available for the CAS mission.

He gave the report and copied down the reply from the JTAC sitting at the FIRES desk. They were launching a flight of two A-10s that were sitting alert at Bagram since there were no other fighters nearby. They would be on station in fifteen minutes. Carpenter breathed a sigh of relief.

"Flight of two Hawgs, sir," Carpenter said, turning to Major Hilton.

"Fuckin'a' right son, good job," Hilton replied as he started to exit the HUMVEE. "Now grab a rifle and your radio and let's kill these sons of bitches."

Carpenter grabbed his rifle and radio and followed Hilton to a covered position behind the HUMVEE. They had set up a 360-degree defensive perimeter around the vehicles as the enemy fighters continued to assault their position. Carpenter made sure his headset was plugged in and switched to the tactical frequency that the fighters would check in on.

Carpenter watched as Maj Hilton moved from position to position, rallying the troops and redirecting their efforts. The man was a "lead from the front" kind of guy. Carpenter respected that about him. He seemed to have no fear at all.

Carpenter took cover behind the HUMVEE as another mortar whistled toward their position. It hit with a thud on the road about forty meters from them and then nothing happened. It was a dud.

"Fucking dumbasses!" Gomez yelled from the turret before unleashing another volley of rounds toward the mortar's position.

"Sandman, Cajun 34 flight checking in," the metallic voice said over the secure radio. Carpenter looked up; he could see two specs circling overhead in trail of each other. The flight of two A-10s had finally made it on station.

Carpenter checked in the two ship with the situation update. He talked them on visually to friendly positions and gave them all the information of the suspected enemy ambush he had. There were two primary ridgelines on the north and south sides of the road where the attacks appeared to be originating. Their main concern was the advancing of the Taliban fighters and overrunning their position before they could make the necessary repairs and get moving again.

Once the orbiting A-10s had their required information, they responded with their fighter to FAC briefing. They were a flight of two A-10s each equipped with five hundred pound laser guided bombs, GPS guided bombs, and 1,350 rounds of 30MM bullets.

"Cajun 34 this is Sandman 41, request a show of

force east to west," Carpenter replied. He was asking the A-10 pilots to fly low over the bad guys' heads to let them know that the A-10s were on station. His hope was that the fighters would realize that they were severely outmatched and flee. It had worked before, and the rules of engagement encouraged it over the use of lethal force.

"Cajun 34 copies, we'll get their heads down," the lead pilot confirmed.

"Cease fire! A-10s inbound!" Carpenter yelled over his shoulder. The guns fell silent as the soldiers echoed the cease-fire command. The soldiers kept concealed as an occasional round plinked off the side of the armored vehicles.

Carpenter watched as the first A-10 rolled in while spitting out self-protection flares. The flares were used to decoy any possible surface to air infrared missiles and were also useful to get the enemy's attention. The first A-10 screamed low overhead at relatively high speed. The whine of its twin turbofan engines was nearly deafening. As it passed overhead, it made an aggressive climbing left-hand turn as it popped out more flares.

The second A-10 was just as impressive as it flew over thirty seconds later. This time, the pilot banked right and climbed, also emitting self-protection flares as it climbed overhead. Carpenter was jealous *That looked fun.*

"America! Fuck yeah!" Gomez screamed, pumping his fist in the air.

Carpenter saw Gomez slump over in the turret before he even heard the register of the round. A sniper had taken advantage of Gomez' carelessness and had hit him in an area not protected be body armor.

As Carpenter sprinted for the HUMVEE door, he prayed it wasn't fatal. He opened the door and reached in. Before he could climb in all the way, he heard a voice behind him.

"Carpenter? What the hell are you doing? I need you working these fighters; you're not a goddamned medic!" It was Maj Hilton. He had managed to appear out of nowhere.

"Gomez is hit, sir," Carpenter said as he tried to grab Gomez.

Maj Hilton grabbed Carpenter and pulled him out of the HUMVEE just as a combat medic arrived. "Do your job. They will do theirs. That's how this works, hooah?"

Carpenter shook it off and pulled out his binoculars to locate the troops on the ridgeline. He found several fighters regrouping as the shooting started again. The fifty on the MRAP lit up behind him as it returned fire.

"Cajun 34, Sandman, advise when ready for first nine line," Carpenter said, calming himself down. He watched as they pulled Gomez out of the HUMVEE and onto the ground to treat him. He had been hit between his collar and the body armor. There was blood everywhere. He was still breathing, but he needed to be evacuated soon.

"Send it," the A-10 pilot said coolly.

Carpenter gave them the required information in the nine line format, reading to them the target location, description, and distance from friendlies. He didn't have his coordinate generating laptop open at the time, so he used a visual talk-on to mark the enemy position.

After the fighters read back the target location and friendly position, Carpenter gave them their attack restrictions. He would clear them to release ordnance once he confirmed they were on the appropriate heading and attacking the right target.

The A-10s took a minute to coordinate amongst themselves and then called ready. They would be dropping GPS bombs using coordinates they generated through their on board sensors.

"Cajun 34 in, heading 360," the first fighter called as he made his attack run.

"Cajun 34, cleared hot," Carpenter replied over the radio.

Carpenter turned toward the other soldiers and yelled, "Thirty seconds!" As before, they echoed the cease-fire and put their heads down. This time, the concern wasn't shooting the low flying A-10s, but getting hit by a stray piece of shrapnel or debris.

As the first bomb impacted the ridgeline, it erupted in a fireball that shook the ground. They were several hundred meters away, but he could feel the hot air on the back of his neck as he hunkered down.

"Cajun 35 in, heading 355," the second fighter

called. This time it was a female voice. Carpenter popped back up to ensure the fighter was indeed pointed at the correct target and not his own position.

"Cajun 35, cleared hot!" Carpenter replied. Again, he gave the troops a "Thirty seconds!" call and they braced for the second bomb. Like the first, it hit on target.

"Good bombs!" Carpenter said on the secure radio.

Carpenter turned to the medic that was treating Gomez. The medics had his helmet off and were talking to him, but there was a pool of blood around him. "How's he doing?"

"He's stable, but we need to get him back on base soon, can you get a medevac?" the medic asked.

"Negative, LZ is too hot at this point," Carpenter said, ducking as another mortar landed on the opposite side of the road.

"Cajun, this is Sandman, advise when ready for next talk on," Carpenter said as he picked up his binoculars to find the enemy mortar position. The shadows from the mountains were making it hard to see as it was nearing sunset. They had been entrenched for over an hour since the IED took out the lead MRAP.

"Cajun 34 ready to copy," the voice replied.

"Call visual friendly positions," Carpenter said.

"Cajun 34 visual," the A-10 pilot replied.

"From the friendly position, the road bends to the north, call contact the bend in the road."

"Contact."

"From our position to that bend, we'll call that one unit of measure. From that bend in the road, move your targeting pod two units of measure to the south and you will see a group of trees near a ridge line."

"Contact. I've got a group of individuals huddled around what looks to be several mortar positions," the A-10 pilot responded.

"Roger, that's your target. Call in with heading, expect clearance on final," Carpenter responded.

As the A-10s set up for their next attack, Carpenter switched to the backup radio and called in the urgent MEDEVAC mission back at the FIRES desk at Bagram. The LZ was currently too hot, but he was hoping that with a few more attacks from the A-10s, it would be clear for the helicopter to land to pick up Gomez and any wounded from the initial IED attack.

A minute later, the first A-10 called in, "Cajun 34, in, heading 200."

"Cleared hot," Carpenter responded. Again, he gave the thirty second call to warn the troops around them to keep their heads down.

As the first bomb hit, shaking the trees and throwing up a fireball, the second A-10 made her "in" call.

Carpenter again confirmed that her nose was pointed at the correct target and called, "Cleared hot."

The second bomb hit the remaining mortar position as the A-10 pulled off target back into its overhead orbit.

"Good bombs," Carpenter said. "Be advised, we have a MEDEVAC mission inbound, callsign Pedro

71."

"Cajun copies. Be advised Cajun 35 is off station to the tanker at this time," the A-10 flight lead said.

"Copy that. Request armed overwatch while we secure the perimeter and ready the patient."

The A-10 pilot acknowledged as he orbited high above. The sun was beginning to set, leaving an orange halo over the ridgeline. It was eerily quiet. The shooting had stopped with the destruction of the mortar position. Carpenter pulled his Night Vision Goggle case out of his tactical bag and prepared them for the upcoming night ops.

"Carpenter!" Maj Hilton barked as he walked up to him. "What's the ETA on that helo?"

Carpenter checked his watch. It had been ten minutes since their proposed launch time. They should be checking in with him in the next five to ten minutes.

"They should be on station within ten, sir," Carpenter replied.

"Good. I'm sending my team out now to sweep the LZ for any IEDs. Let them know to land on the west side. West side only, you got that?"

"Yes, sir."

Maj Hilton turned and walked back to the litter team that was prepping Gomez. When the Pave Hawk helicopter landed, they would meet the Air Force Pararescuemen and hand off Gomez and the other soldier who had gotten shrapnel wounds from the last mortar.

"Sandman, Cajun 34," the lead A-10 pilot called.

"Go ahead," Carpenter responded as he walked back to the HUMVEE.

"I've got several personnel approaching from the northeast on foot, looks to be about a dozen or so."

"What's the range?" Carpenter asked as he pulled out his night optics and began looking in the direction the pilot had just called.

"From your northernmost vehicle, about one hundred meters," the pilot replied.

"Copy, standby," Carpenter responded. He turned and waved for Maj Hilton who was still giving directions to the litter team for their upcoming extract.

"What do you have, Carpenter?"

"Sir, fighters report a dozen individuals in that treeline about one hundred meters northeast. That would make them danger close," Carpenter responded. Due to the possibility of friendly incapacitation and fragmentation injuries from friendly aircraft, declaring an enemy "danger close" required special handling and ground commander initials for the aircraft to employ ordnance.

Maj Hilton paused and considered his next move. The sound of the HH-60 Pave Hawk helicopters became apparent in the distance. They MEDEVAC helicopters would be checking in soon.

"Could be locals or it could be hostiles. If they start shooting, my initials are Sierra Hotel. Otherwise, monitor them and we'll deal with them if they come within fifty meters."

As if on cue, one of the other soldiers yelled, "RPG!" Carpenter and Hilton hit the ground as the rocket-propelled grenade the MRAP next to them, sending sparks and metal fragments everywhere. The gun turrets on the MRAP and dismounted troops immediately returned fire in the direction of the RPG attack.

"Sandman 41, Pedro 71, we're checking in, flight of two, ten miles to the east," the Pave Hawk pilot called over the radio.

"Sandman, Cajun, I'm eyeball the shooter, ready for next nine line, danger close," the A-10 pilot said. His voice had gone from calm to excited. He had just watched the entire RPG attack unfold in his targeting pod video.

Carpenter composed himself as he picked himself up and resumed his cover position behind the HUMVEE. "Cajun, standby. Break break, Pedro 71, this is Sandman 41, we currently have a hot LZ, say playtime."

"Sandman, Pedro, we have thirty minutes of playtime," the helicopter pilot responded.

"Sandman copies, hold ten miles east, hot LZ, standby," Carpenter responded. "Break, Cajun 34, confirm you still have eyes on the shooter?"

"Cajun 34 affirm, they're now at eighty meters and approaching, danger close," the A-10 pilot responded. Carpenter strained to hear his radios over the gunfire around him.

"Copy that, request strafe east to west or west to east, do not overfly friendlies, ground commander initials are Sierra Hotel," Carpenter replied.

The A-10 flight lead read back the initials and restrictions and then set up for his attack. With the mountains on either side, he came in at a low angle and altitude as he readied his 30MM cannon. "Fighters inbound!" Carpenter yelled.

Carpenter watched as the A-10 rolled in parallel to the road and the pilot called, "Cajun 34 in, heading 280."

"Cleared hot!" Carpenter yelled. Seconds later, the rounds hit the treeline as the signature sound of the GAU-8 Avenger gun on the nose of the A-10 growled in his ears. He watched as tree limbs and dirt were kicked up by the massive 30MM bullets.

"Move your bullets twenty meters north, request immediate reattack," Carpenter directed. He wanted to ensure they took out any hiding adversaries as well.

"Cajun 34," the pilot responded as he made a sharp, climbing right hand turn to set up for another attack.

Less than a minute later, the A-10 rolled back in for another attack, "Cajun 34 in, heading 270."

"Cleared hot!" Carpenter responded.

The bullets crackled and kicked up dust again as the A-10 pulled off target, its gun growling as it cycled in the nose.

"Good hits!" Carpenter called.

"Cajun 34 is going to go to the tanker, Cajun 35 is back on station," the lead A-10 pilot said.

"Copy all; confirm Cajun 35 is tally lead's hits?" Carpenter asked.

"Cajun 35, tally target, visual friendlies," the female wingman responded.

Carpenter waited for a moment for return fire. At first, there was nothing but silence. The two gun runs seemed to have worked. Carpenter waited anxiously, hoping it was over.

Just as Carpenter was about to request Cajun 35 return to overwatch, another volley of small arms fire peppered the road and sides of the MRAPs.

"Cajun 35, from lead's hits, walk your bullets fifty meters east, request immediate reattack," Carpenter directed.

The wingman acknowledged and set up for her attack. This time, the A-10 opted to approach from the west for a better angle.

"Cajun 35, in, heading 100," she said as Carpenter watched her wings level.

"Cleared hot!" Carpenter responded.

As before, the A-10 unleashed a fury of 30MM bullets at the target, pulling back up into the overhead orbit after. Carpenter waited for a moment for the gunfire to return. There was none.

"Cajun 35, can you put your sensors back on the last target area and confirm there's no movement?" he asked. He was hoping she could get infrared footage through her targeting pod to confirm there were no further armed individuals.

A few minutes later, Cajun 35 responded, "Previous target area has no movement."

Carpenter turned and gave the thumbs up to Maj Hilton. He was still standing with the litter team as they waited for the landing area to be cleared.

"Pedro 71, you're cleared in. LZ has previous enemy activity, recommend Pedro 72 orbit low cover while Pedro 71 receives casualties."

The aircraft commander of the rescue helicopter agreed and directed the other aircraft to orbit, training its dual mini-guns on the two ridge lines for covering fire in case of another attack. The lead helicopter would be most vulnerable to RPG and IED attacks while on loading the patients.

The lead helicopter came in low and fast, landing just west of the cleared perimeter of the convoy while the other helicopter circled above in a right hand orbit. As its main wheels touched down, the two Air Force Pararescuemen exited with their rifles low and ready.

The litter team led by Maj Hilton approached the two PJs with Gomez as the other medics with the two injured walked closely behind. The lead medic gave the PJ the patient vitals and situation as they carried Gomez to the waiting helicopter. Once all patients were safely onboard, they closed the open side door and lifted off. From the time they landed until the offload, they had only been on the ground for three minutes. Carpenter was impressed.

"Pedro 71 is airborne, clearing to the east," the lead

pilot said over the secure radio.

"Sandman copies, we appreciate the work," Carpenter replied.

With the casualties gone, Maj Hilton focused his attention on getting the damaged MRAP out of the ditch and back in driving condition. Carpenter helped secure the perimeter while maintaining communications with the A-10s overhead.

An hour after the Pave Hawks left with the wounded patients, an Air Force MC-12 checked in overhead with Carpenter. Using their onboard sensors, they were able to confirm that no further enemy combatants were nearby or along their route. They could also find no other hot spots or potential areas for IED emplacements.

With the MRAP wheel repaired and ready for action, the convoy mounted up once again, nearly four hours after their initial stop. To Carpenter, it had felt like much longer. He hoped Gomez was doing ok back at the base.

With Maj Hilton riding shotgun, Carpenter pulled through the gates of Bagram Air Base just after midnight. He had been gone for seventeen hours. To date, it was the longest time outside the wire in his four-month deployment.

"I'm going to go check on Gomez, you can drop me off here if you like," Hilton said as they reached the main road running through Bagram Air Base.

"I'll go with you," Carpenter replied.

Hilton nodded and the two sat in silence as they made their way to the base hospital. After talking to the charge nurse, they found Gomez in intensive care. He had just gotten out of surgery and was sleeping, clutching a picture of his girlfriend. They expected him to make a full recovery, she said.

Carpenter breathed a sigh of relief. He was thankful everyone had made it out alive.

Chloe Moss

Over the Edge

Homestead ARB, FL
15 August 2013
1300L

"To recap, our overall objectives are to kill and
survive," she said as she stood referencing the objectives
written in dry erase marker on the whiteboard behind
her. "We will do this by maintaining mutual support,
one hundred percent valid shots and kills, and timely and
effective offensive and defensive transitions as
appropriate."

She waited as her instructor sitting at the table across
from her finished taking notes. He was an older
Colonel, but he looked much older than he was. His
flight suit hung loosely over his thin frame. His hair was
nearly completely white. A few Lieutenants had joked
that he looked like a World War I fighter pilot raised
from the dead, but none dared say it in front of him. He
was, after all, the Operations Group Commander, and in
charge of all flying operations for the 39th Operations
Group and Fighter Squadron.

"Sir, any questions?" she asked. Her long, curly

brown hair just barely touched her shoulders. She fidgeted as she waited for his response. Capt Chloe "Eve" Moss was briefing her 2 v 1 Air Combat Maneuvering sortie. She and her instructor would go out and practice air-to-air engagements within visual range of their adversary, another F-16. She was nervous since this was her second attempt at flying this flight lead upgrade sortie. Her first had been canceled due to weather, but the brief had not gone well, and her instructor had told her that she would have had to refly it even if the weather had been clear and a million.

After a pregnant pause, Colonel Ross "Coach" Louhan furrowed his wrinkled brow and said, "Is that your brief?"

Moss' face turned red. She felt a panic overwhelm her. *What did I forget? Is he going to no-step bust me?* "Sir?"

"Are you done?" he asked, taking his reading glasses off his crooked nose.

"Yes, sir," she responded nervously. She wasn't sure where he was going with his questioning, but she knew he was trying to call out something she had done wrong. Flight briefings were always ended with a call for questions or clarifications. He obviously knew her briefing was complete.

"What about the AFRC Special Interest Item?" he asked, pointing to the framed piece of paper on the wall behind her. It was an additional briefing item handed down by higher headquarters generally to emphasize safety or another emerging issue among aircrew.

"Sir, that SII does not apply to us," she said timidly. She wasn't sure why it was even on the wall. The current Air Force Reserve Command Special Interest Item reminded aircrew to ensure passengers and cargo were properly secured during flight through moderate turbulence- something a single seat F-16 pilot would not be concerned with.

"It's a mandatory briefing item from higher headquarters," he stated flatly. She wasn't sure if he were just trying to make a point or trying to rattle her. He was definitely succeeding at the latter. She could feel sweat start to bead around her forehead.

"Yes, sir," she said as she turned to read the framed paper behind her. "Aircrew are reminded that while flight into turbulent conditions is not desirable, aircraft commanders should ensure that load masters check integrity of cargo straps and verify that passengers are properly seated and lap belts tight during extended flight into turbulent conditions."

Coach nodded smugly, "I have no further questions. I'll see you at step."

Moss didn't move as Coach picked up his lineup card and glasses and then walked out. She was still rattled from his line of questioning. It was her first flight with him since he had taken over as Operations Group Commander for the 39th. She had only known him previously from what her fiancé, Cal Martin, had told her. He was a former F-16 pilot who had been grounded after an incident in Iraq. Cal blamed Coach for ruining his career, and Chloe was starting to see why. The man lived up to his reputation.

Moss gathered her briefing guides and lineup card and walked out of the briefing room. As she made her way through the long hallway of the fifteen thousand square foot vault, Major "Pounder" Van Pelt, the squadron's Weapons Officer was waiting for her by the vault door.

"Heard you had a rough briefing," he said with a snicker. *Word seemed to travel faster than the supersonic F-16s in this place.* She wasn't surprised. Ever since the squadron had found out that she had picked up an active duty assignment to their reserve squadron, they had been out to get her. She was the first female pilot. *Such blasphemy could not stand in their boys-only flying club.* So they resisted, but they never expected her to push back. They never expected her former U.S. Representative mother to make a casual phone call to the three star at AFRC and politely suggest that a female fighter pilot blazing the trail for others was good for the military and Reserves in general. She had won the battle, but the war waged on.

As she stood there staring at Coach's favorite Weapons Officer and golden boy, she wondered what exactly she had won. Her career growth had been stunted. She was upgrading to flight lead well after her active duty peers, and to make matters worse, they were nit-picking every little thing about her sorties and making her refly the rides. She resolved to not let their hate and jealousy get to her, but it was getting harder by the day. *They never seemed to relent.*

"I didn't brief the SII. It's a required item. I should have briefed it in detail. After all, *wouldn't want to get a passenger hurt during turbulence,*" she said with a straight face.

"Well you're still getting to fly. Don't suck," he replied as he turned back toward his cubicle.

Don't suck. Great advice. Which lesson was that at Weapons School? It was a daily struggle, the cross she bore for being a pioneer. She knew she would show them all one day and the Pounders and Coaches of the world would eat crow. *She was sure of it.*

Moss continued out to life support to retrieve her flight gear. She pulled her hair into a bun and put her G-suit and harness on before stuffing her helmet in her helmet bag. Coach didn't even acknowledge her as he finished zipping his G-suit. Moss felt awkward. *Nice to have a wingman who hates you,* she thought.

"Don't worry, you'll do great," a voice from behind her said. It was Lt Col "Magic" Manny, the squadron's Director of Operations. She had always liked him. His brown eyes seemed to light up at the thought of flying. *He was one of the good ones.*

"Thanks, go easy on us," she said. Magic would serve as the adversary for their sortie. He would simulate an enemy MiG in his F-16 as she and Coach worked together to defeat his simulated missiles and gunshots.

Manny gave a wink and smiled. Moss felt slightly reassured. Unlike other Gators, she knew Magic wasn't out to get her. He would play by the rules and be fair in simulating the enemy. He wouldn't do anything to make her look bad. If it weren't for her wingman, she would've actually felt at ease.

After receiving their step briefing, they walked to their jets on the large, open ramp lined with rows of F-16s. The Gators' fleet of Block 70 F-16s was the product of a creative upgrade program from the current Chief of Staff of the Air Force who found funds to buy AESA radars and a host of other electronic upgrades to modernize an aging fleet of F-16s. The active duty was lucky enough to get brand new jets off the showroom floor in Fort Worth, based on the UAE Block 60 variants, while the Guard and Reserve components were funded to upgrade their Block 30s and 40s to the Block 70 standard. These upgrades included conformal fuel tanks, color LCD displays, and helmet-mounted cueing systems.

Moss returned the salute of her crew chief and shook his hand as she approached her aircraft. After a quick walk around, she climbed the ladder and strapped in. With her pre-flight checks done, she moved the JFS switch to START 2 and the Jet Fuel Starter system whirred to life. As the F-16's big GE engine started to turn, she moved the single throttle from the cut-off position to IDLE and the engine began its start sequence. Once started, she lowered the big bubble canopy and began powering on her avionics.

"Gator 11, check," she said over the primary frequency at the appointed check in time.

After a long silence, she heard, "3."

"Gator 11, check," she said again, hoping Coach would come up this time.

"3," came the reply after another silence. *At least Magic was on frequency*, she thought.

Before she could try another check in, Coach came up on the primary frequency, "Gator 12."

Satisfied that all players were on the same frequency and ready, she called ground for taxi clearance for the three ship. The flight taxied out to the end of the runway. After their flares were armed and final checks accomplished by the End of Runway crew, Moss called for clearance for takeoff.

After a brief delay for a Customs UH-60 Blackhawk to execute an approach, Moss' three ship was cleared for takeoff. They took the runway and took off sequentially in ten second intervals. Coach rejoined in a tactical line abreast formation a mile off Moss' right wing, and Magic maintained a one-mile trail as the stinger.

As they made their way over the crystal blue waters of the Atlantic, Moss checked in with Miami center and they were cleared to work from surface to fifty thousand feet within the confines of Warning Area W-465. After a quick ninety degree, 5G check turn to the left, followed by a one hundred eighty degree 7G turn to the right to ensure their bodies and systems were ready to sustain high G maneuvering, Moss set up the first engagement.

"Next set will be a defensive perch setup," she said over the primary frequency. She and Coach would fly line abreast of each other while Magic would maintain one-mile trail. At the "Fight's On" call, they would assess who Magic was engaging and execute a coordinated defensive break turn. The intent of the exercise was to simulate having a bandit sneak up on them, forcing them to maneuver to defeat any shots, and work together to kill the adversary.

Once they were at the appropriate altitude and airspeed, Moss called, "Gator 11 is ready."

"Gator 12 ready," Coach replied.

"Adversary ready," Magic echoed.

"Gator's fight's on, Gator 12 break right, bogey six o'clock, two miles!" Moss called, seeing the tiny speck of Magic's F-16 directly behind Coach.

Moss tightened her legs and abs as she started the hard break turn to the right. She focused on her Anti-G Straining Maneuver as the force of seven times her bodyweight pressed down on her. As she made it through the turn, she could see Magic's F-16 saddling up behind Coach as he also broke right while ejecting self-protection flares. As Coach and Magic merged, Coach reversed the direction of his turn, forcing the fight away from Moss' jet. It was exactly as she had briefed in accordance with F-16 standard tactics. She checked for a good tone from the captive carry AIM-9 training missile on her right wing and pressed the red pickle button on the sidestick, simulating an AIM-9 shot.

"Gator 11, kill hostile Viper left hand turn, low," she announced over the primary frequency.

"Gator 13 copies kill," Magic responded as he discontinued the engagement.

Moss exhaled behind her mask. Her first engagement had been a quick, decisive kill. It was exactly what she felt she needed after a rocky brief and not being able to get Coach up on comms in the chocks. Her confidence was finally coming back.

Moss set up the flight for another engagement as before. This time, Coach called for her to break left as Magic started at her six o'clock. The setup went exactly according to plan, and as she merged with Magic and reversed her turn, Coach called the kill. Her flight was two for two in successful engagements. She just needed one more and the flight would be a success.

Moss performed an ops check to ensure all fighters had sufficient fuel for another engagement. They were all nearing Bingo, the prebriefed fuel state to go back to base, but they had enough fuel for another engagement.

Once all fighters called ready, Moss called the "Fight's On."

"Gator 11, break left, bogey your six," Coach called calmly. There was no emotion or pitch in his monotone voice. He might as well have been telling her she had something in her teeth.

Moss rolled the jet and began a descending 7G left

hand turn. She tried to look over her shoulder to find
Magic's jet, but was blinded by the sun.

"Bogey switched," Coach called, indicating that
Magic had disengaged from her aircraft and was now
actively fighting Coach. As Moss completed the turn,
she could make out the two F-16s swirling toward the
ocean in a tight spiral. In combat, she could have easily
picked out the F-16 from the MiG, but in training, it was
nearly impossible to tell which jet was friendly and which
was foe.

"Gator 12, status high or low?" she asked. She
could clearly see one aircraft behind and slightly above
the other. She had to be sure before employing
ordnance. A fratricide would certainly be the abrupt end
to her slowly improving day.

"Gator 12 is high man," Coach responded. She
could hear him breathing heavily as he keyed the mike.

Chloe locked the aircraft in the defensive position.
With Coach offensive, there was no need to take the
shot and risk a fratricide.

"Status shot?" Coach demanded. "Gator 12
defensive!"

Chloe was confused. He had called "high man"
earlier, which was clearly the offensive fighter, but now
Coach was calling defensive. She broke lock, fearing
that she had inadvertently locked Coach instead.

"Gator 11, take the shot!" Coach exclaimed.

Chloe locked the trail aircraft and hit the pickle
button, simulating the missile shot.

"Gator 11, kill hostile Viper, left hand turn," she replied.

Chloe's heart sank as she looked at her fuel. She had completely missed her "BINGO" warning and had burned well below Bingo fuel. She needed to climb up and get pointed toward home.

She cleared Coach to rejoin and Magic to get his own separate clearance back to Homestead as she contacted Miami center. She would have to climb up through airliner jet routes to make it home safely, so she declared a fuel emergency. The Miami controller was more than willing to help, and cleared her directly to Homestead at whatever altitude she needed.

After the long descent directly to the field, Moss landed with just under 1200 lbs of gas, well within legal limits. She had been conservative in declaring an emergency, but she was sure that if she hadn't she would not have had sufficient fuel to land safely.

After signing the forms with maintenance and hanging up her flight gear in life support, Moss regrouped with Coach and Magic in the vault to debrief. She found an empty briefing room and cued their Digital Video Recorders to the "Fight's On" of the first engagement.

"Anything for motherhood?" she asked as she started the debrief process. The "motherhood" of the mission referred to the administrative portions that included getting to and from the training airspace.

"You were late on check in," Coach said as he

looked at the notes he had scribbled on his card.

Moss frowned and looked at Magic for support. She didn't want to argue with her instructor, but Coach had clearly buffooned the check-in. She was hoping Magic would intervene, but he looked away in silence.

"And most importantly, you overflew your bingo and then declared an emergency when you didn't need to," Coach said as he pulled of his glasses.

"I was being conservative," Moss replied sheepishly.

"Conservatively over-flying your fuel states?"

"I fucked up, sir," Moss finally admitted.

Satisfied, Coach motioned for Moss to proceed. They went through the first two fights watching the virtual playback of the jets on the debriefing system. Moss' jet was represented by a blue F-16, Coach's jet was green, and Magic's jet was symbolized by a red MiG-29 as they watched the god's eye view of the fights. At the end of each of the first two engagements, Moss wrote down learning points to discuss, but overall, they had gone exactly as advertised. Moss was cautiously optimistic.

They watched the third engagement in real time. Initially, Magic had locked onto Moss' aircraft until switching to fight Coach. Moss' heart sank as she watched the engagement between Coach and Magic play out. The red MiG-29 was defensive the entire time. She watched as her jet turned the corner and locked Magic's jet, only to break lock and shoot Coach's jet. She had committed a blue-on-blue fratricide. Her eyes started to water as she stopped the tape.

"Gator 11 calls a kill, blue on blue with Gator 12," she said. Her voice was shaking. She could see the concern in Magic's face. He was projecting empathy. Coach grinned smugly as he furiously scribbled notes on his card.

"That will be a keg for the squadron bar, and you'll brief this at drill weekend," Coach said, still grinning. "I prefer a dark beer."

Moss held back tears as they went through the learning points of the engagement. She knew Coach had set her up by calling the wrong status, but there was nothing she could do or say to change what she had done. Her only option was to take the sole responsibility so as not to be seen as quibbling. She hated it with every fiber of her being.

As they concluded the flight debrief, Coach cleared Magic off. He gave Chloe an apologetic look as he walked out and closed the door behind him. Chloe took a seat at the briefing room table as Coach stood. She had led the flight portion of the debrief, but now it was time for Coach, as her instructor, to give the instructional feedback.

"Ok, wow, where to begin?" he said with a sigh as he flipped over his lineup card to read the notes he had scribbled.

Chloe said nothing and sat with her pen in hand, ready to take notes.

"First off, your brief. You need to get with Pounder

and work on it. There are mandatory briefing items for all flights. The SII is one of them."

"Yes sir," Chloe responded as she scribbled on her lineup card. She still thought it was utterly ridiculous to brief something that had no applicability to her mission. *No one else in the squadron ever briefed it.*

"We talked about ground ops. You have to start the flight with a commanding presence. Don't fuck up the check in right out the gate," he said as he checked off the second bullet point on his card.

Chloe nodded. There was no pointing in arguing. It wouldn't get her anywhere. She was used to it by now anyway. The whole squadron did this to her when they flew with her.

Coach laughed as he read the next bullet point on his card. "You shot me. That's the first time I've ever been killed by my own flight lead. Make sure you wear your blues when you brief the squadron. Always make sure you positively ID what you're shooting at."

Chloe's eyes welled up. Fratricide was a big deal. She had never done it before, and she had always thought she never would. There was just no excuse for it, even if he had talked her into it airborne. She still was the one that hit the pickle button.

"And finally the fuel issue. That's the part that concerns me the most. You just about ran yourself out of gas and made the Operations Group look bad with Miami Center by declaring an emergency and making them reroute airliners all over the place. Your poor airmanship does not make it ok to just declare an emergency whenever you fuck up. You should never have gotten yourself into this position in the first place." Coach paused for effect. He put his lineup card on the table and took off his reading glasses.

"Now you know, I don't have anything against women flying fighters or even being in the military. I think it's great," Coach continued, "but if this is the performance you're going to give us, you're not living up to the expectations set by those women that have gone before you. No one is going to give you a free pass just because you happen to be a woman. If you can't hack it, maybe you should think about a career in the USO instead."

Coach picked up his glasses and put them in his pocket. "That's all I've got. I'm going to have them take you off the flying schedule for a couple of days. You're going to need to see this flight again."

She sat in the briefing room in stunned silence as Coach walked out. As the door shut behind him, she started to cry.

"*Fuck this squadron,*" she said softly as she wiped away the tears.

An Excerpt from SPECTRE RISING

PROLOGUE

Basra, Iraq
2009

"Thunder 42, Knife 11, standby for new tasking," the secure radio hissed and crackled to life. It was the voice of the British Joint Terminal Attack Controller (JTAC) whom he had been working with for the last two hours.

"Knife 11, Thunder 42, go ahead," he replied, stuffing his water bottle back in his helmet bag. He had been airborne in his F-16 for over four hours, having refueled three times. It was the standard mission in the new Iraq. Takeoff, check in with the JTAC, stare at dirt through the targeting pod for an hour, hit a tanker, check back in with the next JTAC at the next tasking, wash, rinse, and repeat, until the mission window ended six hours later and it was time to land. Not quite as glamorous as the early days of the war where everyone cleaned off their weapons racks on every sortie.

But Captain Cal "Spectre" Martin had never seen that Iraq. It was his second deployment, and despite his air medal, he had always managed to bring his bombs home. He had come close to dropping bombs many times over his thirty combat sorties, usually arriving just as the hostilities were dying down, or being called off because the locals had taken care of the problem already. *The price of success*, he thought.

It truly was a new Iraq. In late 2008, the United States and Iraqi governments came to terms on a Status of Forces agreement. This agreement defined the withdrawal of coalition forces from major Iraqi cities and laid the foundation for their eventual troop drawdown. It also required warrants for searches of any homes and buildings not related to combat. It was the first step of the United States government handing back the keys of Iraq to the Iraqi people.

As a result of this new agreement, however, the rules of engagement for coalition forces became more restrictive. No longer could a JTAC designate a target for destruction based on enemy activity. Search warrants had to be acquired. Iraqi police had to be notified. The remaining airpower, F-16s doing twenty four-hour patrols over predesignated areas, was relegated to searching for suspicious activity through their advanced targeting pods.

And Spectre had been doing just that. He had checked in with Knife 11 to look for suspicious activity - people placing Improvised Explosive Devices on known supply routes mostly. He was number two in a flight of two, separated by thirty miles working with two different JTACs - standard ops with fewer jets to patrol the skies these days.

"Thunder 42, we have a TIC at MSR NOLA, convoy requests immediate support, contact Whiskey 80 on Green 10, how copy?" the JTAC responded in his thick British accent.

He had heard it several times before on his first deployment - TIC, or Troops In Contact, was the magic acronym indicating friendly forces were currently engaging hostiles. Under the current ROE, it was the only way airborne weapons employment was authorized. After hours of lethargy, it was the only phrase that got his blood pumping. Someone on the ground was in trouble, and he was the cavalry. It was his first time hearing it on this tour, and he just hoped he could get there in time to make a difference.

"Thunder 42 copies all, will contact Whiskey 80 on Green 10, copy troops in contact," Spectre replied in an unshakably cool, calm tone despite the adrenaline now coursing through his veins.

"Cleared off, and happy hunting," the Brit replied.

He checked the cheater card on his kneeboard for the frequency called Green 10 and typed it in the upfront control of the F-16. He typed in the coordinates for the center point of MSR NOLA, the codename for the main highway westbound out of Basra. During daylight hours, it would serve as a busy highway for civilian and military traffic, but now at 0200 and with a curfew in effect, it would only be used by the military and those looking for a fight.

Of course, Spectre knew they weren't really looking for a fight. The people still fighting in Iraq were terrorists. They were looking to create fear and panic, and disrupt the progress of rebuilding Iraq. They wanted the infidels out of their land, so they could create a strict Islamic regime that would ultimately be used to oppress the Iraqi people. They were cowards who couldn't win a head on fight with even the budding Iraqi Security Forces. So instead, they played the asymmetric warfare game: ambush the vulnerable convoy with IEDs, harass the American bases with Indirect Fire attacks, and kill the women and children of those who sought to make their country better. It was all part of the desperate last stand of a defeated group.

With his sophisticated Embedded GPS/INS navigation system now directing him to the hot zone, Spectre sped to the area at nearly 500 knots. He knew in these situations time could mean the difference between life and death for the guys on the ground. They were the real reason things were going so well in Iraq, and he wasn't about to let the cowards they were facing get in a sucker punch.

He keyed his auxiliary radio to contact his flight lead. Despite having flown most of the mission alone, he was still the wingman, and his flight lead would be the ultimate decision maker. He needed to get the information to his flight lead as quickly as possible so their firepower would be available to the convoy in trouble.

"Thunder 41, 42 on Aux," he said, indicating that he was calling his flight lead on their secondary radio.

"Go ahead Spectre," he replied. Major Brett "Pounder" Van Pelt was an experienced Instructor Pilot (IP) and flight lead. He had been to Iraq three times prior. He had seen the transition firsthand from the "Wild West" to the restricted "look but don't touch" mindset.

"We've got a TIC at MSR NOLA; I'm inbound to contact Whiskey 80 on Green 10."

"Copy, go check in with the JTAC, I'm on my way, don't do anything without me," Pounder replied sternly. He was a fast burner in the F-16 community, having served as an operational test pilot testing the latest and greatest weapons for the active duty before joining the reserves. Just prior to the deployment, he was even selected by the Air Force Reserve Command as the alternate to go to the coveted Air Force Fighter Weapons School. Pounder was going places.

The convoy was over 50 miles away, but Spectre arrived on scene in just over five minutes. He checked in with the JTAC, callsign Whiskey 80, who gave him the on scene situation. A small convoy had been moving food and medical supplies along MSR NOLA from Basra to a village near Zubayr when an IED exploded, wounding two Iraqi soldiers and severely damaging one of their HUMVEEs.

"Requesting armed overwatch while we move the wounded to the MRAP and repair the HUMVEE, go with Fighter to FAC," the excited voice said over the secure radio. It was Whiskey 80, the American JTAC in the convoy. He sounded young - *couldn't be older than 21,* Spectre thought. *What a shame, not even old enough to drink legally in America, but old enough to have people try to blow him up.*

"Roger, we've got one F-16 with one on the way, each jet with two by GBU-12, two by GBU-38, and five hundred-fifty rounds of 20 millimeter, thirty minutes of playtime. Understand armed overwatch, confirm you're strobing?" he asked, repeating the instructions and giving the fighter to FAC brief, an abbreviated way for pilots to give Forward Air Controllers on the ground their weapons load out and time on station. Tonight each jet was loaded out with two 500lb GBU-12 Laser Guided Bombs, two 500lb GBU-38 GPS guided bombs, and 550 rounds in the 20MM Vulcan cannon sitting over his left shoulder.

"We are now," Whiskey 80 replied, indicating that he had turned on his Infrared Strobe to mark their position.

Spectre took his Night Vision Goggles out of their case and attached them to his helmet. He had been flying all night with them off. He hated them. Unless there was some tactical importance to wearing them, he avoided it at all costs - they just gave him a headache. If there were ever a time of tactical importance, it was now. After a quick scan, he quickly picked up the bright strobe flashing amongst the headlights on the highway. He picked out six vehicles, and then slewed his Litening II Advanced Targeting Pod to their position.

Using the Forward Looking Infrared mode of his targeting pod, he could easily make out the vehicles. The first two were HUMVEEs, followed by three MRAPS - the Army's armored fighting vehicle designed to withstand IED attacks and ambushes, and one HUMVEE at the rear. The black and white pod image wasn't very clear at that altitude, but it appeared that the rear vehicle was the damaged one.

After confirming the JTAC's position, he began scanning the nearby area for threats. He put the jet into a 45-degree bank, right hand turn and set the autopilot to hold that turn so he could focus on the ground. The right hand "wheel" kept the F-16 in an orbit over the target area, keeping the targeting pod that was mounted on the right chin mount from being masked by the fuselage.

Pounder checked in just as he settled into his search. "Do you hear me on secure?" he asked on aux.

"Negative, I'm talking to the JTAC now," Spectre replied.

"I can't hear shit, what's going on?" Pounder demanded.

When he was a Lieutenant, Spectre never appreciated Pounder's attitude, but now it was just flat out annoying. A situation was developing on the ground and for whatever reason Pounder couldn't get his hands in it, so he was being short.

"There's a disabled vehicle and wounded, we're tasked with Armed Overwatch. I'll pass you the coordinates on the datalink, but so far nothing is happening," he said, trying not to show his irritation.

"Sounds like Iraqi standard - hurry up and do nothing. Well I'm almost at Tanker Bingo, so we'll have to yo-yo, think you can handle it by yourself?" Pounder asked. He was nearing the preplanned fuel state to discontinue whatever tactical operations they were conducting so they could make the tanker or go home with enough fuel to land safely. With yo-yo operations, Spectre would stay on station alone until Pounder could get fuel on a tanker and make it back. Once back, they would complete a hand off and Spectre would head to the tanker alone, ensuring a fighter would always be overhead.

"I've still got 20 minutes until Bingo, I can handle it," Spectre replied.

"Fine, but don't do anything without me. I'll be back in 20 minutes."

Spectre acknowledged and continued with his search. He knew the rules. Ever since a young wingman nearly hit friendlies on a drop while his flight lead was at a tanker, the reigning Operations Group Commander had decreed that no aircraft would drop ordnance as a singleton, no matter what the situation. Flight leads were not supposed to leave their wingmen alone on station, but given the situation, Spectre wasn't about to argue and leave these guys alone on the side of a highway in the wee hours of the morning.

"Thunder 42, this is Whiskey 80, we are taking fire!" the JTAC screamed. His voice was cracking. Spectre could hear gunfire in the background. His eyes snapped back to his targeting pod. He could see the friendly troops hiding behind the vehicles on the road. Zooming out the pod image, he picked up two trucks on the other side of the road with several combatants in the back. He couldn't tell what kind of weapons they were holding, but they appeared to be shooting.

"Thunder 42, Whiskey 80, we have troops in contact, danger close, standby for 9 line," he screamed once again. More shots could be heard in the background. They were under heavy fire. The 9 line served as a way for the Forward Air Controller to pass target information in a Close Air Support situation.

Spectre hesitated. He had strict marching orders from Pounder and the rules of engagement - *don't do anything solo*. He could see the friendlies taking heavy fire on the ground. They didn't have the firepower to hold the enemy combatants off by themselves for long, and he had no idea when Pounder would be back. He didn't have time to wait.

"Thunder 42 ready to copy 9 line," he replied. *Fuck it*. He was there to protect the troops on the ground, not watch them die while he sat idly by with his hands tied by ridiculous rules to cover some general's ass.

The JTAC screamed the required information to him and then said, "Request you strafe these fuckers NOW! We're taking heavy fire and they are advancing on our position!"

He had all the information he needed. With the proximity of the enemy to the friendlies, the fragments from the bombs would potentially injure them. He had to be surgical, and the 20MM was his choice. Loaded with High Explosive Incendiary rounds, the bullets would disable any vehicles and rain fire upon the cowards who had ambushed the convoy.

He called up the strafe pipper in the Head Up Display and set the aircraft systems up for his strafe pass. He would make his roll-in parallel to the friendlies so as not to shoot over them or toward them.

His adrenaline was now full throttle. Despite that, he remained focused. He rolled in, establishing a 30-degree nose low dive using the pitch ladders and flight path marker in his HUD. He set the gun cross at the top of the HUD on the target. It was the first truck.

"Thunder 42, in from the east, tally target, visual friendlies," he said, his still-calm voice masking the fear and excitement he was feeling.

"You're cleared hot!" the JTAC replied, indicating Spectre was cleared to expend ordnance on the target.

He steadied the boresight cross on the truck as the gun pipper symbology rose to meet the target. The pipper in the F-16 gave a constantly computed indication of where the bullets would go at any given time. It was commonly referred to as the "death dot" because where you shot, death would follow.

As he reached the preplanned range with the pipper on the truck, he squeezed the trigger. The jet vibrated with a metallic rattle as the Vulcan cannon spat one hundred rounds per second. He held the trigger for three seconds, then released the trigger and began a 5G recovery from the dive.

For what seemed like hours, there was quiet on the radio. He reestablished his right hand wheel and picked up the target again in the targeting pod. He could make out very little as the dust settled from where he hit.

"Good hits! Good hits!" the JTAC exclaimed. "You're cleared immediate reattack on the second truck, you're cleared hot!"

Spectre picked up the second truck visually through his Night Vision Goggles. It was now speeding westbound towards the front of the convoy.

"Confirm the truck is moving to your position," Spectre asked, trying to slow things down so as not to be too rushed and make a mistake.

"That's affirm, he just... oh shit!" the reply was cut off. Spectre's heart sank. He saw the glowing streak of something large and hot shooting from the truck in his FLIR. He knew it immediately. It was an RPG. He watched as the second HUMVEE in the convoy was rocked by the explosion and the infrared targeting pod image washed out from the heat of the blast.

The situation had gone from bad to worse. The radio was silent. He watched helplessly as the truck that had fired the RPG turned back away from the convoy to dig in and continue its assault. He was already risking it, but without a JTAC on the ground, he could not shoot.

"Help!" a scream came over the radio.

"Say again," Spectre asked, hoping it was the JTAC.

"This is the MRAP commander, we are under heavy fire with several casualties, our JTAC is down, request Emergency CAS, my initials are Hotel Sierra!"

Unlike working with a qualified JTAC, Emergency Close Air Support was the most difficult

CAS scenario to manage. It referred to a situation in which a fighter provided support with a ground controller who was not a qualified air controller. Someone with no prior training would be guiding bombs and bullets from fighters onto nearby targets. The rules of engagement allowed it, but only at the discretion of the operator in the air, and only in the direst of situations because of the risk of friendly fire.

He called the MRAP commander back. *Time to go to work*. He confirmed that no personnel or vehicles had moved from the highway. The second truck was still the target.

He picked up the second truck visually and rolled in just like the first time, establishing a 30-degree dive and putting the boresight cross on the truck.

"Thunder 42, in from the west," he said, hoping his new controller would respond.

"Do it! Take them out!" the MRAP commander exclaimed.

He exhaled a bit. At least he had positive contact with someone. Once in range, he put the pipper on the truck and squeezed the trigger for two seconds. The bullets spat from the trusty 20mm just has they had done before until the gun was empty

Just as he began his recovery from the attack, he heard "Abort, abort, abort!" It was the call reserved for discontinuing the attack.

His heart sank.

SPECTRE: ORIGINS

CHAPTER ONE

Homestead, FL
Present Day

Victor Alvarez stood alone in the grass parking lot. It was still dark out, but the horizon glowed orange in the distance as the sun began its upward trek. He hated morning, especially South Florida mornings. The air was almost completely saturated with moisture, and although it was almost fall, it was still eighty degrees.

The parking lot was relatively isolated. It had taken him twenty minutes of driving down a dirt road to reach it. It had previously served as a parking lot for field workers to drop off their vehicles, but with the recent recession and the foreclosure of the landowner, it was now just a vacant lot. He was in an area known as the Redlands of Homestead. Only minutes from the Everglades, it was mostly open farmland with a few houses scattered here and there. It was the perfect place to escape the congestion of Miami, or the eyes of an unwelcome third party observer.

Alvarez leaned against his car as a lone pair of headlights approached from the distance. It was almost six o'clock in the morning. He pulled a handkerchief out of his pocket and wiped the sweat away from his brow. Despite having spent his whole life in this climate, he had still never fully embraced it.

The car pulled to a stop next to his. The silver Honda Civic was much louder than he expected. *It must have a broken muffler or something*, he reasoned. Not quite what he was expecting from a man like the one he was about to meet, but in this business, he had learned not to assume anything, especially not when dealing with Americans.

Alvarez ran his fingers through his jet-black hair and casually approached the car. He was holding a small envelope in his left hand and resting his hand on his holstered gun with his right. The man in the battered Civic was right on time and at the right place, but that didn't make him trust the stranger just yet.

"Are you Victor?" the man in the car asked. It was too dark in the car to make out his face.

"Yes, do you have the documents?" he replied with a thick Spanish accent.

"Here's everything you asked for, flying schedules, personnel files...everything," the man responded nervously, handing Alvarez a thick manila envelope through the car's window.

Alvarez leaned on the roof of the car. He was a tall man, and the low ride height of the car brought the window only up to waist level. He took the envelope from the man and put it on the roof of the car. Alvarez then handed the man the small envelope that he had been holding.

"These are your instructions. The first of the funds has already been transferred. The rest will be delivered upon completion of this operation."

"Oh...ok... uh... But no one knows my name right? There's nothing pointing to me when this is over, right?" The man was fidgeting in his seat.

"Your government will never find out," Alvarez reassured him. "Don't worry."

Alvarez had seen it many times before. He had been an agent with the Cuban Dirección General de Inteligencia for ten years. He had spent most of those years in South Miami. It was easy to blend in there. The majority of the population was Cuban or Hispanic, and almost everyone spoke Spanish fluently. No one even raised an eyebrow. He had used Americans many times before. Occasionally it was for intel, but often it was for assistance. They seemingly always tried to justify what they were doing, whether it was for their families or some political reason. Alvarez didn't care, but he still didn't respect them. He needed them for his operations, but they were traitors to their country, plain and simple.

Alvarez watched as the man opened the envelope and read the instructions. He looked for any signs of hesitation or weakness. He had been assured that his new contact would follow through, but he was more than ready to terminate their arrangement with a 9MM round to the man's temple at the first sign of weakness.

"Do you have any questions?" he asked with a toothy grin.

"No, I can do it."

"Good. Go. You'll be just fine." Alvarez grabbed the files off the roof of the car and pulled out his cell phone as he walked back toward his car. The little Civic sounded like a bumblebee as it sped off into the now rising sun. He dialed the number he had been given by his handler. It was time to check in.

"How did it go?" the voice asked.

"It is done. We have everything we need to proceed." Alvarez knew his cell phone was probably being monitored. The Dirección General de Inteligencia was the main state intelligence agency of Cuba. Since opening for business in late 1961, the DGI had been involved in intelligence and espionage operations across the globe. They had been involved in aiding leftist revolutionary movements in Africa, the Middle East, and mostly Latin America. In the United States, the DGI had been heavily involved with international drug trade, assisting homegrown terrorist cells, and intelligence gathering operations for third party countries. The CIA, NSA, and FBI all had them on their watch lists.

"Excellent. Select the target and do what is necessary."

"Yes, *jefe*. You won't be disappointed." He hung up the phone and tossed the documents on the passenger seat of his car. This was the first operation he had undertaken without the knowledge of his government. It was going to make him a hero and wildly rich. He had a lot of work ahead of him, and a very short timeline.

CHAPTER TWO

R-2901
Four Months Later

"**R**attler 21, Thunder 11 checking in as fragged, ready for words," the metallic voice said over the Harris PRC-117F Manpack Radio. The dismounted radio, called a manpack, served as a multi-band, multimode radio that covered the gamut of waveforms. Frequencies covered included VHF, UHF, and UHF SATCOM radio. The unit was also compatible with the Single Channel Ground and Airborne Radio System, an Army system. It served as a lifeline for any JTAC to support assets in the air.

"Roger Thunder 11, Rattler has you loud and clear, situation is as follows: we have several wounded friendly forces holed up in the urban village. They are unable to move at this time and are surrounded by multiple hostiles in pickup trucks," he replied looking up at the jets circling over their position. From his observation position, he could barely hear the two F-16s in a right hand orbit high above, but with the overcast sky, he could clearly see two dark specks speeding across the clouds like ants on a blanket.

The two men were set up on the roof of a metal building overlooking a series of tin buildings just a quarter mile away. The terrain was relatively flat, and from atop the two-story building, they had a relatively unobstructed view of the village. Even for a village, it wasn't much. A dirt road running north from their observation position was split by fifteen tin buildings before intersecting another dirt road that led out to a narrow tree line.

"Do you recognize the voice?" he asked, turning to the man standing next to him. The man was about six feet tall with a narrow frame and muscular build. He wore khaki 5.11 Tactical pants with a black Survival Krav Maga t-shirt. Oakley Half Jacket mirror tinted sunglasses masked his deep set, blue-gray eyes, and a desert camouflage boonie hat covered his light brown hair. His square jaw clenched as he pondered the question.

"C'mon Joe, you know I don't fly with those assholes anymore," the man replied with a grin.

Tech Sergeant Joe Carpenter laughed and turned back to his Toughbook Laptop and PRC-117 radio. He was wearing the standard issue Air Force ABU digital camouflage uniform complete with flak vest and ballistic helmet. A former Army Ranger, he had been a JTAC for three years after going Green to Blue in search of a more aviation-oriented career. Unable to fly because of a color vision test, his search landed him right back with the Army, as an embedded JTAC.

Perhaps one of the most physically demanding jobs in the Air Force, JTACs were frontline battlefield airmen. They were embedded with ground forces to advise the ground commander on Air Force air power capabilities, and in the heat of battle, to control aircraft during close air support scenarios. Of course, it was just Carpenter's luck that he'd get out of the Army just to go right back in a new uniform, but he didn't mind, he was at the tip of the spear and he loved it.

To Carpenter, though, the best thing about working for Mother Blue was the toys. He knew the Army had the same technology and capabilities, but in the Air Force, he always seemed to have the latest and greatest at his fingertips. At the moment, the latest and greatest happened to be his Toughbook Laptop equipped with the newest Precision Strike Suite for Special Operation Forces software - PSS-SOF. With PSS-SOF, he could pass airborne operators high fidelity GPS coordinates of his own position or the enemy from the comfort of whatever foxhole he happened to be operating out of.

"Damn Spectre, still no love for the Gators?" Carpenter asked sarcastically. The Gators were the 39th Fighter Squadron stationed out of Homestead Air Reserve Base in Southern Florida. One of only two fighter squadrons remaining under the Air Force Reserve Command, the Gators had been Spectre's squadron until the aftermath of his final flight that night in the skies over Iraq.

"None. Don't you think you should pass them a nine line and get this party started?" Spectre was never known for his tact. It was one of many reasons he and Carpenter got along so well.

Carpenter nodded and keyed the microphone as he read from his Toughbook, "Thunder 41, nine line is as follows: items one through three are NA, line four: one hundred twenty feet, line five: group of trucks, line six: One Six Romeo Mike Lima Nine Three Eight Four Four Eight Zero Six, line 7 NA, Line 8: five hundred meters southeast, line 9 as required, remarks: final attack heading 270 plus or minus 10 degrees. Call in with final attack heading and expect clearance on final. Read back lines 4, 6, and restrictions."

The fighter repeated the 9-line perfectly as the F-16s maneuvered into position overhead. By using the standard 9-Line format, Carpenter had given the fighters all the information they needed to take out the target, including elevation, coordinates formatted in Military Grid Reference System, distance from friendly positions and restrictions on attack direction.

"It's Magic," Spectre muttered.

Carpenter turned and gave Spectre a puzzled look.

"Magic? No man, it's science. We give them the coordinates of the bad guys with this fancy laptop, they plug it into their system, and the bad guys go boom."

"No shit smartass, I mean the guy flying. It's Magic Manny," Spectre fired back. Lt Col Steve

"Magic" Manny was the Director of Operations for the Gators.

Carpenter picked up his binoculars with one hand and the handset of his radio in the other as he watched the F-16 roll in on its target.

"Thunder 11, in heading 275," announced the tinny voice of Magic over the PRC-117.

"You're cleared hot," Carpenter replied, clearing the pilot to employ ordnance while ensuring that the fighter's nose was pointing at the right target.

Spectre watched as the F-16 rolled in and hurled itself toward the ground. Seconds later, two objects fell as the jet turned back skyward. He winced in anticipation of the impact only to be greeted by two barely audible thuds.

"Good hits! Good bombs!" Carpenter exclaimed on the radio.

"Inerts are so anticlimactic," Spectre sighed.

"What do you expect? They drop two five hundred pound pieces of concrete that are shaped to look like real bombs. It's way better than when they roll in and just 'simulate' without anything coming off the jet. Now *that* is boring." Carpenter always had a way of putting a positive spin on things.

Just as Spectre was about to explain the merits of training without any ordnance on the aircraft, his cell phone rang. It was his boss.

"I have to go Joe, thanks for letting me spot for you," he said as he hung up the phone.

Carpenter gave him a nod and turned back to the target. He had invited Spectre to make the drive from Homestead to Avon Park to catch up and observe the Forward Air Controller side of Close Air Support. They had been friends since college, but aside from an e-mail or phone call here and there, they rarely got to see each other nearly ten years later.

Spectre picked up his backpack and climbed down the connex container to begin the mile hike back to his truck. His boss had been brief but the sense of urgency was apparent in his voice. It was time to quit playing and get back to the office - *something new had come up*.

With the boss as vague as he was, Spectre was forced to wonder what could be going on until completing the three-hour drive back to Homestead to find out. *Was the store finally going to be bought out by a bigger chain? Did some new, rare find show up that needed an immediate appraisal?* These were the new questions that weighed heavily on his mind since his transition to civilian life.

It wasn't a very easy transition to make. When Spectre was told by his superiors upon returning from Iraq that he'd never fly an Air Force Reserve aircraft again, he refused the non-flying staff job they tried to force on him. For him, flying the F-16 hadn't been about the adrenaline rush or the need for speed. It was about serving a higher purpose. In the current world climate, that meant providing close air support for boots on the ground. When the powers that be decided he was no longer fit to do that, he decided his services could be better used elsewhere.

Unfortunately for Spectre, the economy he escaped to wasn't conducive to his unique skill sets. And after several rejected applications to a myriad of three letter agencies and private contractors, he found himself quickly burning through his savings.

That was until he met Marcus Anderson. The gruff Mr. Anderson had been a classmate of Spectre's in their Survival Krav Maga class. And although Marcus was nearly twenty years his senior, the two became fierce sparring partners. The former Marine versus the former fighter pilot, each did a good job of keeping the other on his toes. A black belt himself, Marcus had helped Spectre earn his black belt in Krav Maga.

Through their training and constant ribbing, the two became good friends. And when Marcus learned that Spectre was down on his luck, he didn't hesitate to bring him in on the family business.

Anderson Police Supply in Florida City, FL was established in 1981 by the late John Anderson. A former Miami-Dade County detective, John Anderson had retired to the more rural Florida City to escape the explosive expansion of Miami and Ft Lauderdale, while still being close enough to visit. What originally started as a hobby of collecting rare and unique guns soon became a fairly lucrative business for John. His buddies from the force appreciated the discounts on firearms and supplies, while the locals enjoyed having a full service firearms dealer with a huge inventory right down the street.

After returning home a decorated Marine Recon Sniper in 1999, Marcus decided to leave the Corps and join his father in running the store. By the time his father passed away in 2001, Marcus had watched the store grow from the back corner of a bait and tackle shop to a 20,000 square foot facility equipped with an indoor shooting range and a fully configurable electronic shoot house.

When Marcus learned that Spectre had a business degree and extensive web design experience from college, he didn't feel so bad about giving Spectre a chance. And after only a year, Anderson Police Supply had become one of the foremost online dealers for firearms and tactical gear.

Spectre arrived at the store well after business hours, but the parking lot was still full. *Something must really be going on*, he thought. He had spent the three-hour drive going over the possibilities in his head, but none of them seemed likely enough to cause

Marcus to be so tight lipped. He really had no idea what to expect.

He swiped his access card and opened the heavy metal door as the lock clicked open. The access control system had been installed shortly after the latest renovations, allowing better control and tracking of those employees who were able to access the building after hours. He then proceeded inside the large showroom, complete with multiple glass showcases. Handguns of all calibers and types were proudly on display inside each case, organized by manufacturer. Rifles of varying calibers and sizes were mounted behind each of showcases on the wall. It was a gun lover's heaven.

Specter noticed the staff crowded around the range rental counter of the store. He could barely make out Marcus' gray hair standing behind it, apparently talking to the staff. He threw his backpack on one of the showcases without slowing down and continued to where the others were gathered around.

"No, it does not mean you'll lose your job," Marcus continued, apparently already midway through his speech. He paused and nodded as he noticed Spectre join the crowd.

"Then what does it mean?" one of the junior salesmen asked.

"Would you let me finish? Do you think I won't tell you?" Marcus barked. The junior salesman retreated, his face red. Spectre chuckled. *That was Marcus.* Patience and diplomacy would never be his legacy.

"What's going on?" Spectre whispered to the girl next to him. She was barely five feet tall with long brown hair and bright blue eyes. To Spectre, and most of the males in the store, she was probably the most attractive girl there. Were it not for his pending engagement, he might have made a move on her. Perhaps even more successfully than the hundreds of guys that were being shot down on a daily basis.

"The boss just announced that the store is downsizing," she replied.

"Downsizing how?"

She replied with a finger to her mouth and pointed to Marcus who was still staring down the junior salesman. Even at 5'9" and just over 170 lbs, Marcus was an expert in creating the fear of God in just about anyone.

"As I was saying," he continued, "we're not downsizing staff for now. We're going to move a lot of the floor salesmen... err... salespeople to the corporate accounts, internet sales, and range. We're also going to be cutting back on the store hours. I don't want to have to let people go, but you're all going to have to work with me. This is the best I can do with the shit sandwich we've been given."

Marcus made a point to make eye contact with every man and woman standing around that counter as if he were readying the troops for a final charge into battle. To Marcus, that wasn't that far from the truth. For his business, this was do or die time. They had to either pull themselves out of the red and adapt to a changing economy, or face extinction.

"That's all I can say for now, folks. Just know that we're going to work together and pull this through. Cal, can I talk to you in private?"

Spectre nodded and walked behind the counter. He followed Marcus into his office and closed the door behind them. Marcus collapsed into his big leather chair and rubbed his temples.

"Nice speech, boss. The troops are ready for war," Spectre poked with a grin.

"War is a lot easier than this shit. *Way easier.* You have a target. You have an objective. You kill him. This? This is a cluster fuck."

"What's going on? When I left yesterday, things weren't so doom and gloom. Sure we had a bad quarter, but nothing we haven't seen before," Spectre replied. He was referring to the quarterly financial reports their accounting staff had put together the day prior. As expected, gun sales were down across the board. The only thing doing well was the internet sales department.

"We were doing fine. Until this morning, and I got this," he said as he handed Spectre a letter.

Spectre took the letter and started reading. He couldn't believe it. It was non-renewal notice from the local Customs and Border Protection branch. One of their largest government contracts for supplying firearms, ammunition, and tactical gear was being terminated.

"I've got a buddy at CBP; I'll ask what's going on."

"Don't bother, I already talked to the Air and Marine Branch Chief in Homestead," Marcus said, eyes closed as if what he was saying was also physically painful, "the President has cut funding to all Customs Air and Marine branches nationwide. He thinks this one might be closing altogether."

"It can't be! This is one of the busiest branches in the country!" Spectre was beside himself. The Homestead Air and Marine Interdiction branch of CBP was the front line in the country's battle against smugglers, drug runners, illegals, and terrorists. With a fleet of Blackhawk helicopters, ASTARS helicopters, Dash-8 surveillance aircraft, and trained interdiction agents, it was second only to the Tucson branch in activity.

"I know. Fucking Democrats." Marcus sighed.

CHAPTER THREE

Homestead, FL

"I love you, I'm just not *in love* with you anymore," she said. Her eyes were watering, but her tone was unwavering and she looked him right in the eyes. There was nothing left for interpretation.

"Chloe, I don't understand. Where did this come from?" Spectre was sitting on the couch right across from Chloe Moss. He was leaning forward, hanging on every word and every gesture from the woman he loved. The woman who, until just seconds ago, he thought loved him too.

"I've been thinking about this for a long time, baby. It's just not the same anymore. You're not the same anymore."

He leaned back on the couch. *Where did this even come from?* They had been together for nearly five years, the last two of which they had been engaged. And despite no firm date for their wedding, he had never questioned their mutual resolve to be together.

"What do you mean I'm not the same anymore? I'm the same man you fell in love with when you first showed up to the squadron. What's going on?"

From the moment they first met, Spectre thought Chloe Moss would be the only girl he would ever love. With her curly light brown hair and bright green eyes,

Spectre was entranced by her the very first time they met at his desk.

"Excuse me, can you tell me where Life Support is? I need to drop this stuff off."

Spectre looked up from his computer in what he'd later describe as a sensory overload. Even in the standard issue flight suit, she was beautiful. Her voice was angelic. She even smelled pretty.

"Huh?" he replied. He was gawking, and a single syllable grunt was about the best he could have hoped for given his surprise.

"Hi, I'm the new pilot here. Lieutenant Chloe Moss," she said, extending what amounted to her free hand as she struggled to hold her g-suit, helmet, and harness with both hands.

He sat there for a second staring at her barely outstretched hand, and then realized what was happening. She was the new Active Duty exchange pilot everyone had been talking about. After regaining his senses, he shook her hand and grabbed the falling harness from her arm.

"Here, let me help you, life support is this way. I'm 'Spectre' Martin. But you can call me Cal. Or Spectre. Or Captain Martin. Or 'Hey You,'" he said with a sheepish grin. *Smooth. Real smooth, Cal. Want to go ahead and tell her the names you just picked out for the children you're going to have too, while you're at it?*

Accepting the help, she followed him to the Life Support shop where pilots kept their flying gear.

"Thanks, Captain Cal 'Spectre' Martin. You can call me Chloe. Or Eve since that's technically my callsign," she said with a wink.

From that point on, their relationship progressed at record pace. Within a few months, just as Spectre was about to deploy on what would be the last deployment of his career, the squadron caught wind of their relationship.

Despite the fact that they were essentially the same rank, and no undue influence existed in their relationship, the leadership was whole-heartedly opposed to their relationship. To them, if it wasn't bad enough that she was the first female fighter pilot, it was worse that one of their own Reservists was dating her. *It could not stand.*

And that began Spectre's downfall with the Gators. As the leadership pushed back, he refused to yield. What he was doing wasn't illegal, and they had determined that they were in love. To Spectre, separation was not an option. The squadron leadership even threatened to have her reassigned, and they would have too, if not for a political favor called in by her mother, the former Congresswoman.

Despite the squadron pushback, their relationship seemed to press on stronger than ever. Spectre deployed with the squadron that had become very much against him while Chloe stayed home and continued her initial upgrade to become a Combat Mission Ready Wingman.

After being sent home early from Iraq, Chloe and Spectre even took it a step further, opting to move in together with their two dogs. Their relationship continued to speed along as they became more and more committed to each other.

And although Chloe continued to fly and slowly make progress with her career while Spectre awaited the outcome of his now famous strafing incident, the two never let it get between them.

Spectre supported her as she struggled through the upgrade program. The squadron seemed to have it out for her, determined to make it painful for her to upgrade. She had reflown several of the upgrade rides and her instructors had threatened a few times to have her pulled from the upgrade program to give her more time in the jet before trying again.

Spectre helped her prepare and study for every flight, giving her advice on how to deal with the squadron that had turned its back on him, while Chloe listened patiently and gave him advice while he relived his own life changing moments over and over.

It had been a tough decision to let it all go, but with his career behind him and the Generals giving him a firm "hell no" on returning to the jet, Spectre decided to move on to civilian life. He would not lose

Chloe and his career. He could manage moving with her every three years. He liked the stability the relationship gave him. So he finally proposed.

Now he was sitting on their couch staring at the ring he had given her as she twisted it around on her finger. It had been his mother's ring. His father had given it to him after she had been killed in a car accident. It had been his grandmother's ring before that. It was the greatest gesture of love he could think of at the time.

"Cal, I love you, but the spark is just not there anymore. You and I have grown apart, and I don't think you even know who you are since you quit flying," she said. She was no longer looking at him, but staring at the ring as she twisted it on her finger.

"So what does this mean? You're done? It's over? You're the one! We can make this work!" His eyes were starting to water.

"I'm sorry baby, but I just don't think so," she replied with a tear rolling down her cheek.

"I thought I was your symbolon, remember? Doesn't that mean anything to you?" Spectre pleaded. It was a nickname Chloe had called him since the day he proposed. It was a term coined by Plato referring to two halves yearning to be joined as one. However, as Spectre asked the question, he realized she hadn't called him that in a while. *Maybe they really were growing apart after all.*

Chloe frowned. She pulled off the ring and looked at it. Time seemed to stand still as she offered it to Spectre.

"Just like that?" he asked. His face felt flush and his heart sank as he took the ring from her.

"I'll sleep in the guest room until we figure out what we're going to do with the house," she offered as she wiped away the tears. Her tone had suddenly turned very business-like. She got up and walked past him, pausing to touch his shoulder. He grabbed her hand.

"It's for the best," she said. She withdrew her hand and walked into the bedroom, closing the door behind her as her Golden Retriever followed in trail.

Spectre sat there, head in hands, trying to digest what had just happened. Zeus, his 100 lb German Shepherd, slowly approached and nudged his elbow with his nose. The dog sensed the pain, and was trying to cushion the blow the only way he knew how.

"What the fuck just happened, Zeus?" But there were no explanations for Spectre, not even from the incredibly perceptive former military working dog.

*****

"Mom, I did it. It's over," she said holding the cell phone to her ear as she collapsed on the bed. Her voice was trembling as she tried to hold back the flood of tears.

"Good for you sweetheart. He wasn't good enough for you," Maureen Ridley responded. Her voice was flat and unemotional.

Chloe sat up and rubbed her bloodshot eyes with her free hand. Her mom had never liked Cal, but Chloe had always thought she'd eventually come around, especially after Cal solidified their relationship with his proposal.

"Mom, I know you didn't like him, but this is still hard," Chloe said. "*Everything* is hard right now."

"Sweetie, you're young. You will find the right guy," Maureen responded reassuringly.

Chloe hesitated for a minute. Part of her wanted to let her mom know about her secret, but she still wasn't quite sure what was going to happen and she was afraid what her mom might say. *It was all such a blur.*

"Thanks mom. I just feel overwhelmed," Chloe finally responded after a long silence.

"Is the squadron still giving you trouble?"

"Every day is a new battle, just like you told me it would be," Chloe replied. As a Congresswoman, her mom had seen firsthand what it was like to be a successful woman in a male dominated profession. It was a constant uphill battle.

"Do I need to make more phone calls?" Maureen asked.

"No, mom, it's fine. They're just doing it because I'm the first female fighter pilot. I won't let them get to me. I'll show them."

"That's my girl," her mom responded. "You'll get through this like you've gotten through everything else. I'm proud of you."

C.W. Lemoine is the author of *SPECTRE RISING*, *AVOID. NEGOTIATE. KILL.*, *ARCHANGEL FALLEN*, and *EXECUTIVE REACTION*. He graduated from the A.B. Freeman School of Business at Tulane University in 2005 and Air Force Officer Training School in 2006. He is a military pilot that has flown the F-16 and F/A-18. He is also a certified Survival Krav Maga Instructor and sheriff's deputy.

http://www.cwlemoine.com

Facebook
http://www.facebook.com/cwlemoine/
Twitter:
http://www.twitter.com/CWLemoine/

Blog:
http://cwlemoine.blogspot.com

Made in the USA
Monee, IL
13 November 2019

16737512R00076